What Would We Do Without You?

A Guide to Volunteer Activities for Kids

BETTERWAY PUBLICATIONS, INC.
WHITE HALL, VIRGINIA

Published by Shoe Tree Press, an imprint of
Betterway Publications, Inc.
P.O. Box 219
Crozet, VA 22932
(804) 823-5661

Cover design and cover photographs by Susan Riley
Typography by Park Lane Associates

Library of Congress Cataloging-in-Publication Data

Henderson, Kathy
        What would we do without you? : a guide to volunteer activities
for kids / Kathy Henderson.
            p.   cm.
        Includes bibliographical references.
        Summary: Examines various services provided by young people
on a volunteer basis in such areas as public health, social services, and
general community service, and discusses how to get involved and be
a better volunteer.
        ISBN 1-55870-152-4 : $6.95
        1. Voluntarism--United States--Juvenile literature.
[1. Voluntarism.] I. Title.
HN90.V64H46   1990
361.3'7--dc20
                                                                    89-29938
                                                                         CIP
                                                                          AC

Printed in the United States of America
0 9 8 7 6 5 4 3 2 1

For my grandparents, Cleo and Aline Davidson,
who, by example, taught me the value of giving.

Acknowledgments

This book would not have been possible without the generous cooperation and support of many people throughout the country. Old friends and colleagues were quick to answer my requests for leads and opinions and advice. New contacts offered their support without hesitation, often forwarding statistics, program information, additional research materials, and photographs without charge. I will be forever grateful to them.

I especially want to thank the young people who shared their experiences as volunteers with me. All were most humble about their efforts and truly believed they gained as much, if not more, from the people and projects in which they were involved. Also, their candid remarks about the occasional problems and conflicts they encountered provided needed balance to the book as a whole.

I'm grateful to the many adults and organizations who encourage volunteerism by young people and work so diligently to provide them with both new opportunities and deserved recognition. And I'm grateful to those in the media who consider "good" news and deeds worthy of report coverage.

For their special contributions and assistance I'd like to thank Tobin Smith, Jill Meisenheimer, Dr. Alice McCarthy, Sheila Cowing, Dwanye Breashears, Jackie Arnold, Mark Sparks, Susan Walter, Judy Erickson, Karen Skrivseth, Cathy Sullivan, Megan Lott, Daphne Hutchinson, Kevin O'Brien, Dennis Stover, Ann Ray, Roberta Alexander, Julie Mullikin, Judith Zazula, Cissy Gaes, Ken Melius, John Dooley, Mary Donovan, Suzanne McKellar, Howard Hogan, Grace Wiegers, Maureen Hosty, Representative

Bob Traxler, Representative Jim McCrery, René Shack-elford, Mary Lynn, Vicki Rakowski, Ann Lutz, Dan Miller, Greg Ferriby, Virgil Strickler, Sheryl Matthews, Donna Vitiello, Helen Johnson, Cheryl Tevis, Betsy Frees, Ardyce Czuchna, Paul Howell, Robert H. Giles, Stephen Butz, Jane Quinn, Ray Jurczyk, Sharon Fritz, Colleen Kaltz, Robert Eager, Rebeccalynn Staples, Grant Carmen, Reverend Buck Switzer, Rosalie White, Elizabeth McGonagle, Neil Emerald, Mike Hyer, Terry Modglin, Sandy Crooper, Sharon Davis, Barb Barlow, Janet Grant, Linda and Larry McNamara, Kathleen Wall, and Nancy Watta. Joyce McDonald, my former editor, also deserves special recognition for her work on this project.

Lastly, I'd like to offer my undying gratitude to my family for pitching in when my time or energy was in short supply; to my neighbor and friend Joan Hansen for her clerical assistance; and to the folks at Betterway—Bob and Jackie Hostage, Susan Lewis, and Susan Sweet—for their support of this project, editorial excellence, and supreme patience and understanding.

Contents

Volunteers Wanted

VOLUNTEERS WANTED: Enthusiastic Young
People Willing To Help Others. No Minimum
Age. Work In Any Field. Thousands Of Positions
To Choose From. No Prior Experience Neces-
sary. Rewards Unlimited. Please Hurry. We
Can't Get Along Without You.

Does an ad like this interest you?

Good. But that's not surprising. Thousands of young people all over the country are already actively volunteering in more projects than ever before. From neighborhood clean up squads in low income housing developments in Minneapolis to drawing soil test samples on crop lands in Kansas. From digging latrines in Latin America to calling bingo games at nursing homes in suburban New Jersey. From door-to-door canvassing for political candidates in Connecticut to sponsoring a needy child in an Ethiopian village. From providing positive peer pressure to help classmates stay in school in downtown Detroit to cleaning litter from trout streams in Virginia. From raising puppies for Leader Dogs to collecting newspapers and cans for recycling nearly everywhere. And everywhere they go, they are appreciated. Young volunteers have become needed, sometimes essential, parts of many organizations.

Over and over, young volunteers hear, "What would we do without you?" Volunteers—kindergartners through teens—come in all sizes and colors, with abilities and economic backgrounds and ethnic heritages as diverse as the

Members of New Orleans's Audubon Zoo Corps act as EdZOOcators for zoo visitors. (Used by permission of the Audubon Zoological Garden.)

projects themselves. However, all volunteers share some very special traits. They have energy to spare, a curious nature, plus ideas and hobbies that get them excited. They care about the people and world around them. But most of all, they share a willingness to get involved for the good of others, the community in general, and the world at large.

Are you one of them? If not, you could be.

Whether you are a beginner looking for your first project, or a seasoned volunteer looking for new challenges, you'll find advice and resources here that will help you tap new opportunities, widen your horizons, expand your knowledge, and develop new and varied friendships. You'll meet a variety of young volunteers, kids just like you, and learn firsthand how and why they got involved. You'll also learn about the benefits that you can gain through volunteerism, and what to do when it's time to move on to a new opportunity. More important, you'll learn that participation can help you develop a greater sense of self-worth by seeing how each of us can and does affect the world we live in.

Finding activities is easy. The more you look for ways to volunteer, the more activities you'll discover, because wherever there are people, there are jobs to be done, causes to support, money to raise, and someone in need of help. The hard part comes when you have to choose among the hundreds of opportunities available.

The projects featured in this guide represent only a handful of the opportunities available to young people. They were selected not only for their diversity, but also as examples of the types of activities to look for, or start, within your own community. By studying basic program guidelines as well as individual requirements and restrictions, you'll get a realistic view of what you can expect from a similar program.

TAKING A LOOK AT YOURSELF

Never volunteered before? Don't worry, getting involved is easy even for beginners, no matter how old or young they are. All you have to do is be willing to participate.

But before you jump into a project, take a look at yourself. If you have goals you want to accomplish, if you would like to make the world a better place to live in, then do some serious thinking before selecting which volunteer activities you want to be involved in.

The following questions will help you make choices not only as an active volunteer but in many other areas of your life as well. Since we're not always sure what we truly think about a situation until we see it in black and white, you might find it useful to write down your answers. Then you'll have them to refer to in the future.

What do I believe in?

What priority does it have in my life?

Which causes do I feel strongly about supporting?

Am I familiar with any current programs or projects that address these issues?

Do I know any of the people involved? Does it matter?

What are they doing to help?

Is it helping?

Is it something I'd be willing to do?

Am I currently contributing to this cause in some way?

Does this project require a long- or short-term commitment?

Do I have time to make a positive contribution?

Am I willing to make time?

Am I interested in developing skills that would help make me a good volunteer for this cause?

What skills, abilities, or special interests do I currently possess that would be useful to this cause?

Would it help to know more about the cause itself, the subject matter, and/or the program and people involved?

Would I rather find a different way to contribute to this cause? What are my choices?

Are there any reasons to say "no" to this project?

How would contributing to this cause affect the rest of my life, my friends, or my family?

The answers to these questions are very important. We have so many demands placed on us throughout our lives—through school and work, and by family and friends—that it's easy to get swept away in directions we find out later we really didn't plan to follow.

Once you've analyzed your goals, you can start looking for ways to accomplish them. You may have decided to do what you can for the environment. Or it may be that you want to volunteer to help the disabled. Whatever your goal, there are ways to be of service.

The easiest way to start may be to join a club or organization that already is involved in volunteer projects that interest you. But you don't have to join a club to become a volunteer. If you want to come up with a volunteer activity on your own, or form your own club with friends, be sure to read Chapter 4. With that chapter, plus some brainstorming with your friends or family, you're sure to find a worthwhile way to help.

If you decide to work with an established group, a short term project is an especially good way for a beginning volunteer to start. Join a local youth organization such as Boy or Girl Scouts, 4-H, Camp Fire, Boys and Girls Clubs, or YMCA, to name just a few, or a club at school. Each encourages members to participate in at least one service project a year. Most have set procedures to follow and a project guaranteed to be successful, so you won't have to worry about coming up with all the ideas on your own. Plus, they'll be glad to have your help. If you don't already know someone involved, ask your school secretary, neighborhood librarian, clergy representative, or teacher for help. Also watch the local newspaper and listen to a radio or TV station in your area for announcements of upcoming community events.

Some groups, especially those with national ties, are

more visible than others. It may take a little digging to uncover some worthy yet smaller organizations. Don't feel you need to join the first club you find. Take some time to learn what each offers. Ask if you can attend a couple meetings before you officially join to see how things are done, and what will be expected of you. Judith B. Erickson, author of *Directory of American Youth Organizations*, also recommends asking current club members about their involvement. Among the questions she suggests are:

Why did you join this organization? What first got you interested?

How long have you been a member?

What do you like best about this organization?

Is there anything you don't like about it?

Does this organization hold regular meetings? When and where?

What usually goes on at a meeting?

Has belonging to this organization made a difference in your life? How?

What are some other advantages of being a member?

Why do you think people should join this organization?

And once you become involved as a volunteer, evaluate your goals occasionally. As you learn and grow and experience new things, your interests and priorities may change, sometimes a little, sometimes a lot. That's okay. Change is a natural part of growing older. Learning to react positively to it will help keep you in charge of your life. And when you're in charge of your life, there's nothing you can't do. Just ask a successful volunteer!

Finding the Groups
that Need You

USING THIS BOOK

You're looking for something to do—a service project, a cause to support. Maybe you want to do something with your club, or maybe something all by yourself. You want something challenging, but fun, something exciting, but worthwhile, too. But what?

Or maybe you know the area you're interested in, but you don't know how to get involved. You really want to help, but you don't know what opportunities there are for someone your age. Will they let you in the door?

In the chapters that follow, you'll learn about a wide variety of activities which use volunteer support from young people. The activities have been grouped into seven primary interest areas: community, health and hunger, peer support groups, animals, the environment, political awareness, and international, with a chapter on each. Please note, however, that within each category you will also discover references and examples of activities which could have also been listed in one or more other sections, or may even have deserved a chapter of its own. I have made a particular effort to show how various activities can be tailored by groups and individuals to meet particular needs or interests.

Each chapter begins with profiles related to that category. Some profiles give insight into an activity from the volunteer's point of view, while others present background information about an organization with an overview of the volunteer activities open to young people. At the end of each profile are suggestions for locating similar opportunities, as well as places to look for more information and resources. Following the profiles are the names and addresses of other organizations that either directly sponsor activities which rely on volunteer help, or regularly encourage their members to volunteer for related activities. Additional organizations and resources are listed in the Appendix.

Bear in mind as you read each profile or listing that it may highlight only one or a few of that sponsor's many projects and volunteer opportunities for young people, and that many activities fall into one or more categories. For some activities, age and experience requirements are only guidelines, while in others, sponsors have strictly enforced age restrictions.

BE PERSISTENT

Megan Lott, organizing director for the National Teen-Age Republicans, is just one of many program directors who urges young people who are truly interested in a particular opportunity to be persistent. "Of course you don't want to be seen as a pest," warns Lott. "But persistence shows a degree of active dedication. A young person who expresses a sincere desire to contribute will be respected for his or her persistence."

Her advice is particularly relevant to young people who are anxious to volunteer in areas where policies regarding young volunteers may limit, or even prohibit, their involvement. While you may not be able to get policy changed, a sponsor may offer you an opportunity in a nonrestricted area where you will have a chance to learn more about the field. Eventually, as your knowledge and skills grow, you may well earn a promotion to the area of service you are most interested in.

Suzanne McKellar, who calls herself a roving volunteer because she helps in a number of departments at Canine Companions for Independence, agrees with Lott. Young people who are really interested in working at CCI and appear responsible might be allowed to volunteer despite their young age and lack of experience. "They certainly wouldn't be turned away," says McKellar. However, she also points out that very young volunteers would probably not be allowed to work directly with the animals at first. Instead, they might be asked to work in the front office stuffing envelopes or helping with the newsletter. Still, says McKellar, they would be in a position to learn a great deal about the program firsthand, including how both the dogs and new owners are trained to work with each other.

Your interest in a profile from this book may lead you to try something similar in your area. If you live in Austin, Texas, and it's the Congressional aide activity from Chapter 10 that interests you, why not find out if your own state capital can use you in a similar way?

Remember, just because a 4-H club in New Jersey sponsors a special "prom" night for mentally retarded persons, that doesn't mean a community service club in Mississippi can't do the same. One of the major objectives of this book is to share examples of successful projects. Adapt these ideas for your own purposes or use them as springboards for completely new projects. Notice that many activities are actually projects within projects, such as the many local fundraisers that bring in funds to support a larger project. Feel free to mix and match ideas from various sources.

Also, use the activities described here to identify similar projects within your own area. For instance, nearly every community has an animal shelter of some kind where you can volunteer your services. You might also see what positions are available through your city zoo, neighborhood veterinarian hospital, or pet store. Who takes care of the various classroom critters like mice, snakes, or fish at your school? Where do they go during holidays and summer vacation? Do your neighbors own pets that you can help exercise or care for during emergencies?

If you are really interested in helping animals, rather than just getting a chance to pet or play with them, then be willing to file papers, stuff envelopes, sweep floors, or clean out cages, if that's where your help is needed most.

The volunteers who get a chance to assist staff trainers and caretakers for organizations like Canine Companions for Independence usually earn the right by first proving their dedication through their willingness to perform less glamorous chores as needed.

If you are truly interested in serving in a specialized field or at a particular position, keep in mind that being accepted as a volunteer is not like attending school. No one has to make a place for you. However, if you are willing to start at an entry level position, you have an excellent chance of reaching your ultimate goal. Many young people find that volunteer activities lead them into fulfilling, longtime careers.

THE FIRST STEP: YOUR OWN COMMUNITY

Well-established youth organizations are among the best places to start looking for contacts, ideas, and resource materials. The address and the person to contact for many of them are included here. You can find additional contacts in *The Directory of American Youth Organizations*, by Judith B. Erickson. However, most program directors of national organizations suggest looking first for a resource person within your own community. A parent, teacher, school counselor, clergy representative, or friend should be able to help you contact the organization you are interested in. And if no local group currently exists in your area, the national organization may willing to help you start one.

If you know the name of the organization, you can check the white pages of your phone book. Look, for instance, under "Boys Clubs" for the center nearest you. Check your local county government listing under "Cooperative Extension Service" for the nearest 4-H agent who can then direct you to clubs of interest in your area. If you don't know the exact name of the group, try looking under "Associations", "Clubs", and "Organizations" in the yellow section of the phone book. Your local United Way office will also be able to direct you to various projects and clubs in your area.

4-H members in San Francisco share the fun of farm animals with city dwellers. (Used by permission of Paul Hennes.)

Many areas of the country also have agencies which serve as information and referral centers between those wishing to volunteer and the businesses and organizations hoping to recruit them. These centers are sometimes known as "voluntary action centers" or "volunteer clearinghouses." The Volunteer and Information Agency for Greater New Orleans is an excellent example of one such group. As of October 1989, over 460 organizations were listed with this Louisiana agency. Approximately 145 organizations welcome volunteer help from those eighteen and under. These young people can volunteer not only in such traditional settings as hospitals, nursing homes, and cultural centers, but also in some less frequently thought of locations such as the Bureau of Governmental Research and the Internal Revenue Service. Other volunteer outlets for young people in the area include the Audubon Park and Zoological Gardens, the American Civil Liberties Union, the Historic New Orleans Collection, and the National Conference of Christians and Jews. During peak summer months, the group refers as many as 400-500 young volunteers (mostly high schoolers) to area projects.

On a national level, Youth Service America serves as one of the major clearinghouses of public service resources and volunteer opportunities for young people. They work particularly with schools and colleges and through the offices of mayors and governors. YSA estimates that within their service and conservation programs alone, young people volunteer over 250 million hours of service each year at a financial worth of one billion dollars. At just the high school level, YSA estimates 341,000 students contribute 17 million hours of service annually at a worth of $59.5 million.

If your school or community is not currently affiliated with YSA, contact them directly at their national office: Youth Service America, 1319 F St. NW, Suite 900, Washington, DC 20004, (202) 783-8855.

A wide range of volunteer opportunities is also available to young people through other groups such as the Volunteers of America, Inc. However, programs vary considerably from one post to another, and VOA representatives advise interested young people to contact their local VOA office, if one exists. The local number can usually be found in the phone book.

LEARNING FROM OTHER GROUPS

There are some activities, like sponsoring a needy child through a world health organization or mowing an elderly neighbor's lawn, which you can plan and carry out all on your own. Other activities, like recycling projects, work better when a family or all the members of a club pull together.

But many times, to transform a volunteer activity idea into a successful project, cooperation between two or more groups of people work best. One example is a Boys and Girls Club organizing a beautification project at a community park with members of a women's garden club. Another example is a student council which collects clothes or food for the needy that is then distributed by the local fire-fighter's association. Sometimes everything from planning, funding, and people power is contributed equally. Most often, however, each group supplies the best of what it has to offer. For instance, in the example above, the garden club may purchase the plants and flowers themselves and help decide where they would look best, while the members of the youth club may do the actually digging, planting, and cleaning up.

Volunteer groups can often learn from each other such basic how-to information as how to keep records, recruit volunteers, evaluate both project ideas and outcome, put together action plans, and estimate budgets for proposed projects. Do you have questions about one of these topics? Call another volunteer organization to find out how they have solved the problem.

"Don't think you have to re-invent the wheel with each new project," advises one volunteer. There is a lot of help available. For instance, the Republican National Committee has a Working Partners' Solutions packet. Free on request, it is a hefty collection of newspaper clips of successful community service projects, plus examples of actual press releases and program action plans that cover everything from planning timelines to dealing with the media. Of special interest to young volunteers is a community partnership workbook called *Neighbor Helping Neighbor* that is an easy to follow, five step guide and notebook for planning a simple community service project. With adult guidance, this guide is ideal to help even kindergarten students plan a project.

ADDITIONAL RESOURCES

A simple way to find seemingly hidden resources is to always ask for additional names and phone numbers when you call to request basic program information. Also be on the lookout for newspaper and magazine articles with how-to advice. Even if it doesn't apply to a current project, it might prove very useful in the future.

In addition to helping kids their own age, Junior Guardian Angels also visit nursing home residents. (Used by permission of Junior Guardian Angels.)

Future Farmers of America test water quality at a local farm. (Used by permission of Successful Farming.)

To make sure you can locate collected information when you need it, start a resource file for yourself or your group. An easy method to keep track of loose papers is to photocopy or clip articles as you find them, note the source, slip them into clear sheet protectors (available at your office supply outlet), and store in a sturdy, loose-leaf binder. Be sure to include a "table of contents" sheet that lists in one place everything included in your file. That will save you from sending for duplicate information, or for searching for an article or information you don't have. Since how-to methods sometimes change, and organizations frequently add or discontinue programs, each entry should also state when it was published or filed. This will help you decide when it's time to send for updated information.

Now when your club suddenly decides to hold a yard sale to raise money for, say, "Jerry's Kids," you can refer to an article like "How to Organize a Tag Sale" and have a basic action plan ready in minutes with expert advice to guide you from pricing merchandise and setting up to where best to advertise.

Many times, whether you are organizing a project just for yourself or as part of a group, you'll want to know more information about a specific subject itself. Again, many national youth organizations can help. You may have even collected information and stored it in your resource file as described earlier.

However, you might want to also check *The Encyclopedia of Associations*. This comprehensive reference book is updated annually and is available in most public libraries. (Due to its high cost, some libraries may only purchase new editions every second or third year. But even an older edition is an excellent resource.) Check under headings such as *social, education, youth, international*, and *service* for information of greatest interest to young volunteers. Each listing includes general information about the association, such as when it was founded, the number of active members, the purpose for which it was founded (the association's goals or mission statement), and often the availability of various materials including newsletters, reports and speakers. Be sure to skim through other sections, too. You'll be amazed at how many organized special interest groups there are in the world! If they don't have the specific background or historical information you want on hand, in most cases they will be able to direct you to an alternative source of information.

If you are interested in a volunteer project that you can combine with a vacation, check your library or bookstore for *Volunteer Vacations,* by Bill McMillan. While a majority of the activities are only open to older teens and adults, there are many opportunities in which younger volunteers can participate if they are part of a youth group or accompanied by a parent or guardian. Many of the activities cited are located overseas or at state and national parks throughout the United States. The activities are very diverse, ranging from working on historic railway lines in Great Britain or archaeological digs in the Middle East to participating in whale research off the Washington and Alaskan coasts. *Mobility International USA,* located in Eugene, Oregon even helps place people with disabilities in volunteer positions both in the U.S. and abroad. Anyone over fourteen may apply.

McMillan also publishes a newsletter called *Volunteer Vacations Update.* For subscription information and a complimentary copy write to: Bill McMillan, Volunteer Vacations Update, 2120 Greenhill Road, Sebastopol, CA 95472.

Exploring Careers Through Volunteerism, by Charlotte Lobb, (Richards Rosen Press) is another resource worth checking out, especially if you're a teen who'd like to work in a field that you are thinking about pursuing professionally in the future. Though its listings are a bit dated (the book was published in 1976) it will, nonetheless, give you an overview of a wide variety of career-oriented positions.

There is also help from the U.S. government. Among the free or inexpensive pamphlets (less than $2.00) available through the United States Consumer Information Center are: *How to Create a Kidsummit Against Drugs* with detailed instructions, forms, and resources to help organize students in fourth grade and up to stop drug abuse; *Take Pride in America with Mark Trail,* a coloring book that teaches children how to take care of our wildlife and public land; and *What to Do When A Friend is Depressed: A Guide for Students.* You can pick up a free catalog of available publications at many public libraries, post offices, and government buildings. Or write: R. Wood, Consumer Information Center-N, P.O. Box 100, Pueblo, CO 81002

REQUESTING INFORMATION

Whenever you request information, make sure that the person or organization you are interested in knows exactly what type of information you are requesting. Do you want general information about the program or organization? Do you want them to send all available program materials directly to you, or should they go to the club president or adult leader? Do you want information just for yourself or family? Or do you want enough brochures to pass out to everyone in your club?

Do you want to be referred to a local source? Are you volunteering now, or just thinking about it? Do you want an application form? Are you trying to verify an organization's credentials? Do you have questions about a program that aren't answered in materials you have already collected? Do you want help planning or implementing a project? Are you in the middle of a project and confused about what to do next?

Your letter doesn't need to be long and drawn out. But the clearer you can be about what information you'd like to receive, the quicker and more helpful the response will be that you get in return.

It is also a courtesy to let the person or organization know how you learned about their program. Did you read an article or advertisement about them in a newspaper, magazine, or book? Did you learn about it in school? Do you know someone who participated in the past? You may want to add a bit of information about yourself and why you are interested in learning more about the program.

In general, be polite, get to the point, and close. Here are two sample request letters:

April 6, 1990
12 Oak Street
Allentown, Pennsylvania

Muscular Dystrophy Association, Inc.
G-6054 1/2 Fenton Rd
Flint, MI 48507

Dear Program Director:

Our Student Council is interested in raising funds for MDA by sponsoring a carnival at our school this fall. We would like to receive one of the MDA carnival kits that were mentioned in an article we read in our local newspaper.

Please send the kit directly to our council advisor, Mr. Hudson, at the address below. We would also like to learn more about muscular dystrophy so please send any additional information that will help us. The phone number at our school is (313) 555-0000.

Thank you.

Sincerely,

Kerry Clarke
Secretary, Mayfair Student Council

SEND INFORMATION TO:
Mr. Steve Hudson
Lehigh Elementary Student Council
27 Second Avenue
Allentown, PA

November 22, 1990
20 Palm Drive
Tucson, Arizona
(602) 555-0000

Student Conservation Association, Inc.
P.O. Box 550
Charlestown, NH 03603

Dear Mr. Howard:

My name is Bob Griffin. I'm in the seventh
grade and learned about your conservation
program from one of my teachers at school.
Spending time during the summer at a national forest and helping to plant seedlings
sounds like something I'd like to be involved with. I'd like to learn more about
your program and how I can sign up.

Please send any available information to me
at the address above. My phone number is:
(602) 555-0000.

I'm looking forward to your reply.

Sincerely,

Bobby Griffin.

WHERE'S MY LETTER?

Most organizations respond to requests for general program information within one or two weeks. If you call and
make your request, you'll sometimes receive information
the very next day. Occasionally, however, it will take as
long as four to eight weeks, or even longer, before the

mailman delivers a packet. On rare occasions, you'll receive no reply at all. Occasionally, organizations close down for lack of funding or people, or they may merge with another group.

When you're excited about a project, waiting for a reply can seems endless. Why is it taking so long?

A response may be delayed for several reasons. Often organizations are understaffed, receiving many more requests than their workers, often part time, unpaid volunteers themselves, can respond to on a daily basis. Sometimes an organization will be temporarily out of material to send. Or they may be in the process of updating their information packets and feel a delay in responding is worth being able to send you the most up-to-date materials available. Then again, your request may have been lost in the mail or, unfortunately, misplaced at the office.

There is another reason you may not receive information. Surprisingly, it happens more often than people realize. People simply forget to include a return address with their request. Don't laugh. As an active volunteer for many projects, I've lost track of the number of times I received a rumpled envelope with no return address and a scrawled message inside that says: Please send info. Nothing else. Not even a signature. Sometimes the request is specific, courteous, and neatly typed. Yet, somehow, they overlook saying where to send the packet. Most frustrating are the times when people order special items and include cash or a money order, but forget to include a return address. I wonder what these people must think of us for taking their money and then never filling their order!

Here are some suggestions to help make sure nothing like that ever happens to you:

Always type or neatly print your address on both the mailing envelope and on your note or letter inside. If you include a mailing label that you have addressed to yourself, the organization can simply stick it to the packet they are sending you.

An alternative solution appreciated by many individuals and smaller organizations with tight budgets, especially when you are requesting a personal reply and not just general information, is to enclose a self-addressed, stamped envelope, known as a SASE.

To prepare a SASE: Address a second envelope as if you were mailing yourself a letter (a #10 business size is best). Stick on a first class postage stamp. For the return address use the individual or organization's name from whom you are requesting information. Then place this second envelope inside your original mailing envelope along with your request for information. If you expect to receive several sheets of information or a pamphlet or brochure, you may want to include additional postage on your SASE to help meet postage requirements.

By enclosing a SASE you are saving the organization the cost of postage and actually making a donation to the group. One stamp may not seem like much of a donation. But think of the savings when a hundred or more people a year each include a self-addressed, stamped envelope.

If you don't receive a reply within a few weeks, and you are still interested in the program, call or send a follow up letter mentioning that this is your second request. If you didn't do so the first time, give a telephone number where you or someone in your group can be reached in case the staff wants to ask any questions about your request.

You might also want to send your request to a second location. For instance, if you requested general information from the national headquarters, call or write the district or regional office. If you couldn't get all the answers you wanted from a regional office, write directly to the program director at the national headquarters if one exists. But remember, like volunteering itself, contacts are best made and maintained on a local level whenever possible.

VOLUNTEERING

If you are already a member of an organization that regularly sponsors community service projects, all you need to do to get involved is raise your hand and say, "I'll help," then show up at the proper time and place as promised. Personal projects, however, will depend entirely upon your own dedication and commitment to follow through on a schedule that you have designed for yourself.

Sometimes, however, the process of volunteering is more complicated. You may need to fill out an application form, just as if you were applying for a regular job. You may be asked to supply recommendations and a resume. You may be asked to write a personal essay about why you want to volunteer. You may be asked to come in for a face-to-face interview. The next chapter will help you work your way through each step of the process.

3.

Handling Applications and Interviews

THE APPLICATION

To participate in some volunteer activities, whether on your own or as part of a group, you first have to fill out an application. Some are very simple forms on which you just fill in your name, address, phone, birthdate and so on. If you are younger than eighteen (under twenty-one in some states) the form might also ask for a parent's or guardian's signature to show that you have their permission to participate.

Most likely, there will be a place for you to sign your name, too. This shows that you understand the type of project you are volunteering for. Before you sign, be sure that you do know enough about the program. Have you asked what your responsibilities will be? Do you know when to report and for how long? Are there any costs that you have to pay, such as for a uniform or transportation and meals? Does signing this application put you directly into a project, or is it a preliminary application that needs to be approved by an organization or individual before you are accepted as a volunteer?

The time to study all this is before you sign, not after. Most disappointing volunteer experiences can be avoided if you know all the facts beforehand. Also, it's not fair to other volunteers to say that you'll help, only to drop out later when you find you aren't really interested, can't afford to continue, or simply don't like the activity you have agreed to perform.

PERSONAL EXPERIENCE ESSAYS

In addition to standard information, you'll often be asked to explain why you want to participate in a particular project. You may also be asked additional information about your lifestyle. For instance, the Helping Hands program, needs volunteers to raise baby monkeys that will later be trained to help the disabled. They need to know the following:

Why you wish to become a foster parent

A description of your pet history

The number of people in your household and their ages

The number of hours you can devote to the monkey each day

If you work outside of your home, information on other persons who would be spending time with the monkey

A letter answering these types of questions is basically an essay, similar to the ones you write for school assignments. It's important that you be honest about your background, experiences, and why you want to get involved. Many project coordinators stress that volunteers shouldn't try to appear as if they know more than they really do. To be a willing and eager learner is often more important.

Write your letter or essay in a conversational tone. Use action nouns and verbs as much as possible. Back up any experience claims with pertinent and concrete examples.

For instance, if you hope to provide a foster home for an animal, you'll want to include the chores you have done regularly (and without nagging!) for a personal or family pet. Have you cared for an injured wild animal before? Participated in obedience training classes in the past? Because you must return all foster animals to the program after a certain length of time, you may also want to mention how you handled a similar experience, like the death of a pet, or returning an wild animal to its natural environment. You may want to share other experiences such as hosting an exchange student in the past or being part of a foster child program.

In an application to a summer camp for the disabled or to a hospital aide program you may want to include first aid classes you've taken or experiences you've had dealing with a disabled friend or family member. Even your experiences as a hospital patient yourself might be pertinent, especially if you remember how good you felt when a volunteer dropped by for a few minutes.

Sometimes, a well written letter is the only opportunity you'll have to apply for a special volunteer activity. This is especially true for projects that may not have allowed young people to participate in the past. Kathleen Wall, assistant site supervisor for the Plimoth Plantation living history village in Massachusetts, says, "We can tell a lot about a child from his or her letter."

While no one will be grading your letter or essay in the same way a teacher would, take time to do a good job. You want to give a good impression, and your essay will often take the place of a face-to-face meeting. Make an outline of the things you want to include. Write one or more drafts. Revise and polish. Check your letter for spelling, grammar, and punctuation errors. An error free letter shows you care about details. Then rewrite or type a clean final copy. It will be worth the effort, especially if you are competing for a limited number of available positions. However, always remember that you are applying as a potential volunteer, not necessarily as a journalist. Write in friendly tones using everyday words. Be positive. Don't put yourself down. (No lines like: I know I probably don't have a chance of being accepted, but I would like to be a volunteer at Mayfair Hospital.) Let your personality shine through.

INTERVIEW HOW-TO

Sometimes the selection process will include a personal interview, especially if you will be working with the public in your volunteer position. There are two secrets to a good interview. One, be prepared. And two, be yourself.

Even if a personal essay isn't required as part of the application process, write one for your own sake. It will help you organize your thoughts, assess your previous experiences, and evaluate your reasons for wanting to become a volunteer. Don't memorize a speech, but be prepared to answer a variety of questions. And listen to the interviewer. You may even want to practice an interview with a friend. Take turns being the interviewer and the person being interviewed.

"My advice is to try not to be nervous. Just be yourself," says Ann Ray of the Children's Museum in Indianapolis. The museum uses as many as 500 volunteers each year, some as young as ten. An interview is a frequent part of the general application process and always a part of the appointment process to serve on the Youth Advisory Council. Ms. Ray adds, "I know that being nervous is a natural part of it. But the kids who impress me the most are the ones who feel comfortable with what they know and don't try to show off or try to be more than they really are.

"We all learn our whole lives long, and you don't need to know everything. There's a whole lot to be learned from everything and everyone you come in contact with."

John Dooley, director for Camp Fantastic expects his teen applicants to "display poise and creativity. And they should feel free to ask questions. Taking the initiative to make the interview a two-way dialogue instead of an interrogation and looking the person in the eye—those are things I strongly suggest." Mr. Dooley adds that an applicant shouldn't act like a "victim" during an interview. Plus, "Dress is still important whether we like to think so or not."

For more advice about filling out applications and surviving personal interviews, consult a book such as Rose P. Lee's, *A Real Job for You: An Employment Guide for Teens* (Betterway Publications, Inc. 1985).

4

Just Do It: Volunteering on Your Own

INDEPENDENT ACTION

Not all projects require advanced planning or help to carry out. In fact, many can be classified as "just do it's" and are great if you want to work on your own or form a club with a few friends.

For example, you can help the environment by keeping trash picked up at your neighborhood park. You don't need official permission. You can put trash in bins right at the park, or if they always seem full or are spaced too far apart, you can bring along some trash bags and ties from home. You may even want to buy or borrow a pair of latex gloves to protect your hands. Filled bags can be left next to the park's regular bins for collection.

You can make a special trip to the park or just spend a few minutes to an hour picking up on one of your regular visits. Best of all, you can make this project a lifetime habit, picking up litter whenever you see it, even if you're not working on a specific cleanup project. And, of course, you can help by never being a litterbug yourself. Friends who normally toss their empty soft drink cans into the nearest bush, will think twice if you nonchalantly walk by a trash can and drop your soda can in. It's a great way to exert a little spur-of-the-moment positive peer pressure. Your individual contribution may not seem like a lot, but when a lot of individuals "just do it," the contributions add up to a cleaner world for us all.

High school student tutor demonstrates a physics experiment to younger kids.

Picking up litter from parks and wild areas can be an independent project as well as a group one. (Photo by Cathryn Berger Kaye. Used by permission of the Constitutional Rights Foundation.)

To help further, you can become more conscientious about the types of products you buy or use. For instance, request paper instead of plastic shopping bags at the grocer. Even if you don't have access to a recycling center, you can recycle bags by taking a few back to the store to refill each time you shop. Styrofoam egg cartons won't decompose in the local landfill for hundreds of years, but you can use them again to start seedling plants or for any number of craft projects. And, like shopping bags, you can recycle them if there are local farmers who could reuse them.

To be an effective recycler, you must also be willing to buy products manufactured from recycled materials whenever possible, especially those made from glass, metal, or paper. Watch for symbols on packaging that identify it as being made from recycled materials.

Shopping for a Better World is a guide available from the Council on Economic Priorities that rates the makers of over 1600 brand name products and helps you choose products to buy which are safer for the environment. The Council also has a variety of other resource materials and suggestions that can help you "just do it" everyday.

If you do have access to a recycling center, start sorting and saving recyclable goods at home. You can also sort the bottles and cans that you collected at the park. Experiment also with other ways to recycle products on your own. Shipping envelopes, especially fiber or plastic filled ones, can easily be reused. Inexpensive notepaper can be made from the backs of unneeded report, typing, or stationery paper. And the comics section of the newspaper makes a fun gift-wrapping paper.

Look through your closet for little used or outgrown clothing in good condition that you can donate to the Good Will, Salvation Army, local Red Cross disaster aid unit, or church ministry project. Give some thought to who will be wearing your donated clothes. Warm coats, hats, scarves, mittens, boots, and sturdy shoes are always in demand, especially in the northern states. Lighter weight but practical clothes are needed for summer or in warmer climates. Consider organizing a yard or garage sale and donate the cash proceeds to your favorite charity instead.

Recycle worn or outdated clothing and fabric scraps by stitching quilts to give to emergency shelters or the homeless, or donate them to a school fundraising bazaar. Even if you don't sew yourself, you can donate items or scraps to a church or group that does. You can provide an additional service by asking someone how to sort the material by fabric type and weight or offering to remove zippers, buttons, and other trim.

Individual projects aren't limited to conservation and environmental awareness. You don't have to be part of a group to volunteer your services at a neighborhood nursing home or hospital. Use your imagination to help raise funds for a local charity or other nonprofit group. Tutor a friend who needs help with a school assignment. Volunteer to mow an elderly neighbor's lawn. Write letters to the media and your government representatives on issues that concern you. Take a first aid course so you are prepared for an emergency.

Helping teens with special needs is rewarding in itself, but it is also good background for a career in special education, occupational therapy, or recreation. (Photo by Cathryn Berger Kaye. Used by permission of the Constitutional Rights Foundation.)

Nearly all projects traditionally done by a group, can also be adapted for "just do it" projects you can do on your own. If you have an idea, follow it through.

You Don't Need a Big Organization

Many of the young people in this book started projects on their own without the backing of a big organization. Jason Gaes, in Chapter 7, wrote his own book about cancer because he felt there was a need for it. Mitchell Vitiello started visiting rest home residents because he was looking for a new project. And Howard Hogan started his own teen Republican Club because he couldn't find a young people's group that shared his values and goals.

You can use many of the ideas in this book without joining the group that is described here. Or you may not know of a group that shares your concerns. Perhaps you're interested in doing what you can to preserve the world's tropical rain forests. Follow the lead of Janet McGinness, in Chapter 11, who used her school newspaper as a way to educate others about world affairs. Or invent a board game that can be used to teach kids about the world importance of these forests. The world peace game described in Chapter 11 has had quite an impact. The more people who learn about an issue, the more people there will be to contribute time and money. Learn all you can about the problem that interests you. Then you can decide what to do. You'll know whether to volunteer on your own, donate your time to an existing group, or raise money to help solve the problem.

Read the profiles in this book of kids' whose stories interest you. Then read the "You Can Do It" section that follows. There you'll often find suggestions on how to begin a similar project on your own.

Raising Money

There are lots of ways to earn money. You can babysit or do odd jobs so that you can make a personal contribution. If you've formed your own group at school, you have more options. You can always have a car wash, but you have some more original choices, too. What about one of these?

- ❏ Have a book swap. Collect used paperback books from other students. Then set up a table in the cafeteria to sell the books for a quarter apiece. (You can give each person who has donated two or more books a coupon for a free book.) It's a good idea to have the sale right before Christmas so that books for younger kids and adults can be sold for use as Christmas presents.

- ❏ Sell refreshments at a school fair, dance, book sale, or other event. Or, if your school is used as a polling place at election time, sell baked goods to the voters.

- ❏ Rent out the club's services for a day. Be ready to wash windows, mow lawns, and clean out basements. Send out notices to let community people know that they can "Rent-a-Student" for a day's work at a set fee. Make sure people know where the money will be going. You'll get more business once people know their money is going to an important cause.

- ❏ Run a day care program one Saturday each month. Hold it at a church or community center that is convenient for shoppers. Parents with errands to do will appreciate it, and you'll earn money.

5.

Community Service Projects

MUSEUM GUIDES

Each year approximately 500 young volunteers work at The Children's Museum, located in Indianapolis, Indiana. Ann Ray, a master teacher says, "They are an integral and important part of our entire program."

Volunteers, who may be as young as ten, start by signing up for the MAP, or Museum Apprentice Program. It is so popular that there is often a long waiting list of applicants. Every six months, the museum sponsors an orientation time when everyone on the list comes into museum. They are shown around and introduced to all the various activities that are open to them. Volunteers can select which gallery or project center they would like to work in. Among the choices are physical or natural science, history, culture, and computers.

After selecting an area, volunteers attend training sessions related to their special subject. Though each area has different displays and features, all volunteers are asked to work with the public within their various areas. For instance, in the natural science gallery, they may give cave tours in the center's built-in cave or play a game of Fossil Concentration with the public. They might be in charge of the snake talks, which means they take the snakes into the mini-science area and do actual presentations about snakes.

A young volunteer works with a visitor in the Computer Discovery Center. (Photo by Ed Lacy, Jr. Used by permission of The Children's Museum.)

Or they might become "Mr. or Ms. Pockets" and serve as moving displays. Walking through the museum in multi-pocketed white lab coats, these volunteers pull things out to show and discuss items that are related to natural science. Volunteers also help clean cages and take care of the exhibit animals.

Ms. Ray points out that a brand new volunteer wouldn't be in charge of such projects right away. "When you first start off, you might shadow somebody and see how they do their job. As you acquire more skills, you can work your way up to other activities."

It is skill, not age, that determines volunteers' responsibilities. "Of course," says Ms. Ray, "the more they come in to volunteer, the more skills they learn."

New volunteers in the computer center, for instance, start out by taking tickets at the door, cleaning monitor screens, or restocking printers with paper. Then they work their way up until they have shown that they have acquired skills in a certain area. "I ended up with volunteers who were actually writing programs," says Ms. Ray, who ran the computer center for five years. "One volunteer even designed a program that helped keep track of all the volunteers within our center, so that when they came in, they could log in on the computer and log out when they went home. The program also kept track of the total hours each volunteer worked."

In most of the galleries, displays and programs are designed and produced by adult staff members, although young volunteers do have some input into various activities. "The kids are having more and more input as we become more of a museum with children and not just for children," says Ms. Ray.

In addition to volunteering in the museum, experienced volunteers may be recommended as members to the twenty-five member Youth Advisory Council, which was started three years ago. It, too, is open to children as young as ten.

Appointment to the council is based on how well a volunteer has worked with the public and his or her understanding of the museum in general.

The council, which meets monthly, is more than just an honorary group. "They really do advise," says Ms. Ray. "We have exhibit teams that come to the council to ask their opinions on concepts that are being worked on. People from the gift shop have asked the council for their ideas on what types of products to stock."

In the past, council members have also served as ambassadors from the museum in various activities around the city. For instance, in 1989, they attended a conference for mayors at which they described the museum and explained their firsthand involvement.

You Can Do It

Area young people interested in volunteering should contact The Children's Museum, Melody Plew, Youth Co-ordinator, P.O. Box 3000, Indianapolis, IN 46206, (317) 924-5431. Adults interested in initiating similar programs in their areas may contact Mike Hyer, Media Relations Coordinator for the Children's Museum at the above address or call the public relations department at: (317) 921-4003.

The Children's Museum in Indianapolis is only one of many science and cultural centers that encourage active participation by young volunteers. Check museums, historical societies, and cultural centers in your area to find out about ongoing projects or to suggest starting a youth volunteer corps. Many living history centers such as Plimouth Plantation and Old Sturbridge Village, both in Massachusetts, Mackinac Island located in the Upper Peninsula of Michigan, and Colonial Williamsburg in Virginia also offer limited volunteer opportunities for youth.

KIDS FOR KIDS, A DANCE FOR A DANCE

Several years ago, after some 4-H members in Monmouth, New Jersey discovered that the developmentally disabled young adults with whom they were working had never had a chance to attend a prom, they decided to plan one for their special friends themselves.

They went to their local 4-H Junior Youth Council, who approved the idea but didn't have any money available to help fund it. Undaunted, the kids decided they could raise the needed money on their own by sponsoring twenty-four-hour dance marathon they would call: Kids for Kids—A Dance for a Dance. They would collect pledge donations from throughout the community based on each hour they planned to dance.

The event proved so popular with marathon participants, both 4-Hers and nonmembers, that it became an annual event in itself. Each year it raises thousands of dollars to fund an annual prom for the area's developmentally disabled. The project, coordinated through the local Association for Retarded Citizens (ARC), is unique in that retarded youth help run both the dance marathon and the prom with the 4-H Kids for Kids club members.

Over the years, the New Jersey 4-Hers have won numerous awards for their efforts, including for three years in a row the Congressional Award for Community Service sponsored by Senator Bill Bradley, and the national ARC service award at both the state and national level.

In 1989, the project grew almost too large to handle, drawing nearly 300 prom guests from throughout New Jersey, as well as areas in neighboring Pennsylvania and New York. "For the first time," says Cathy Sullivan, one of the club's co-leaders, "we had to turn down one of our special friends. And that broke our hearts. We had already moved in two additional tables. No one was seated except the special guests. We simply could not accommodate another person."

For 1990, the club decided to move the prom to a larger facility. They also decided they needed to seek out new members to add to the club's core group of about twenty-eight, because an age gap was forming between very young members and seniors who would be leaving. "You can't have a year where the oldest kid is thirteen or fourteen," says Sullivan. "Because then who's going to lead the group? These kids really do this themselves. They plan menus. They plan the marathon. They plan everything. This is such a big commitment that most of our members belong to just this one club and their only projects are the marathon and the prom."

Despite the club's popularity and the generous community support it attracts each year, it nearly folded in 1988, when the club's original adult leader decided she couldn't continue any longer. But it was the 4-Hers who again who took charge and sought a solution.

"All on their own the kids called a parents' meeting and said, 'What are you going to do about this? This is too good, you can't let it die,'" recalls Mrs. Sullivan. Then she laughs. "They were quite persuasive in suckering all the parents into helping."

Christine Sullivan, seventeen, is the club's current president. Her involvement began six years ago when she volunteered to raise money in the marathon. "I went to the marathon because I knew it sounded like a lot of fun, and that was all I was really interested in at the time. But because I was one of the top ten money raisers, I got the chance to go to the prom.

"At the prom, I suddenly realized what the money was going for and how happy these people were made just by our dancing and putting this prom together. I found I couldn't just leave it. So I ended up joining the 4-H Kids for Kids club."

Each year, Christine says, the project gets a little bigger and harder to do. And as she's gotten older, she has taken on more responsibilities. "It takes a lot of effort and a lot of coordination from all the members." She admits that it's sometimes also a lot of hassle.

"But when you can be with the guests at just one special dance like this, the look on their faces is more than enough repayment. At the end, the band plays the theme song, "You Light Up Our Lives," and some of them are so happy, they're crying. I know some of the moms are crying, and some of the 4-H kids, too. It's an incredibly emotional experience. Knowing you've been a part of it makes it all worthwhile."

You Can Do It

Christine has advice for other kids who want to plan something similar. "When you first get involved, make sure you are very, very organized. And make sure you deal with the special guests not as if they are people who are totally different from yourself. Just treat them as people. You can't be afraid of them because they sense that. You'll loosen up around them really quickly."

The group has found that it's best to coordinate the project with a local ARC, because they will be aware of any special problems involving the retarded. The ARC will also help locate potential guests for the prom by publishing an announcement in their newsletter. Also, the club warns, it's best to start small.

The 4-H Kids for Kids club has a detailed packet available for those who want to plan a similar project. It includes information on planning and carrying out the marathon as well as the prom, sample menus and budgets for each, plus advice for interacting with special guests. Mrs. Sullivan adds that if someone is really interested, she'll help take them through it step by step. To help defray costs, send a large, self-addressed stamped envelope to: 4-H Kids for Kids, P.O. Box 768, Middletown, New Jersey 07748. Or call the club's special phone number: (201) 291-7551.

NURSING HOME VOLUNTEER

Mitchell Vitiello, fourteen, of Fort Wayne, New Jersey, got involved with his special project in a most unusual way. "Basically I volunteered because I couldn't have a dog," he says and then laughs.

Before he started his volunteer work at the nursing home, Mitchell had adopted a stray dog. "Everybody knew the dog and liked him, but he didn't have a home," Mitchell says about the husky-beagle he named Chester. "He was great." But after three years, Mitchell's allergies became so bad, even with Chester living in the garage instead of the house, he had to get rid of him.

Mitchell really missed Chester, and when his mother suggested that he get involved with a new project, Mitchell decided he might like to visit people in a nursing home because of how much he loved visiting with his elderly aunt and uncle who now live in Florida.

"They tell these great stories about their history, where they grew up, what work they did," explains Mitchell. "I love hearing it all. And I like watching their faces. You know, they are so expressive." Mitchell can't stop himself from adding, "Besides, I was sure I wouldn't be allergic to the people at the nursing home."

Mitchell's story about his dog is just part of a growing comedy routine he now shares during his weekly visits to the Oakridge Manor Nursing Home. According to Mitchell, he doesn't plan the jokes, but they just come

Mitchell Vitiello calls bingo games for a neighborhood nursing home. (Used by permission of Mitchell and Donna Vitiello.)

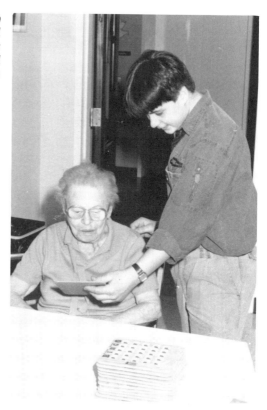

naturally, popping into his head and out his mouth while he calls the bingo games each Sunday afternoon.

"Every week I do the same joke when I pull out the little B-4 ball. Instead of just saying 'B-4' I always pause and add 'and after.' And every time it cracks them up. Most of them have short memories. I don't think they remember that I did the same joke the week before. If they do remember, they'd probably be disappointed now if I left it out."

Mitchell has been making regular visits to the nursing home for over a year. Everyone looks forward to his coming, and not just because he keeps the popular bingo game going. He genuinely cares for the residents, worries about them, and enjoys being with them.

Each week after setting things up, Mitchell goes around the building announcing the game and getting the residents to come. "You know," he says. "They are really lonely. Sometimes they just sit there with nothing to do, no one to talk to. They need to be touched. And I feel wanted there, and they feel wanted back."

Unlike Mitchell, many people feel extremely uncomfortable visiting with older people even if they are relatives. Many people are also uncomfortable communicating with others who have emotional or physical handicaps. They worry that they won't know what to say or do. Mitchell worries sometimes, too. But he doesn't let it stop him. He knows what it's like to be shunned by people who are put off by old age or a medical handicap. He suffers from Tourette's Syndrome, a movement disorder that is caused by overproduction of dopamine in the brain. Sometimes called "tic disorder" it causes involuntary body movements and, depending on the severity, various other problems such as loud swearing in public. Mitchell's symptoms were worse when he was younger but are now considered relatively mild. Still, he has never forgotten how people acted when his problems were worse.

"When I had Tourette's real bad, people used to look at my appearance—my head jerking—and not pay attention to me. The people at the nursing home never notice that I jerk my head sometimes, or swing my arms. They just see me."

You Can Do It

There are nursing homes, long-term medical-care facilities, and senior citizen housing projects in nearly every community. Most welcome friendly visits by volunteers of all ages.

Like Mitchell, you might be asked to coordinate a special project for residents. Members of Junior Guardian Angels in Minneapolis plan regular Saturday visits to a nursing home where they play cards, sing songs, or just sit together and talk. Some of the residents are so delighted by the visiting Angels that they offer to help sponsor them by donating money to help pay for their uniforms.

Other youth groups, such as Scouts and Pioneers, often perform special presentations, like short plays or Christmas carols, at local centers during holidays. They frequently make gifts to share with each resident as well. Still others, like the Ridgefield, Connecticut, Young Republicans, have a permanent offer to perform various services for seniors throughout the year. In the past they have cut and raked lawns, delivered groceries and prescriptions, and escorted seniors to appointments.

While organized visits by youth groups are nice, what nursing home residents enjoy most are visits by young people who just come to say hello and have a friendly chat.

It's best to discuss your plans with the administrator or program director before your first visit. He or she can tell you how their facility is run, what activities may already be planned, and which residents would benefit most from a visit by you. This is one activity where no previous experience is required—just the willingness to be a friend.

LAW ENFORCEMENT EXPLORERS

Exploring is a program developed by Boy Scouts of America. While some Explorers may also be Scouts, the Explorer program operates as a separate phase of the organization and is open to both boys and girls.

Through the Explorers, teens can actively participate in

career fields which interest them. They can also perform important volunteer work in their communities.

According to Dan Miller, executive director for the Boy Scouts' Blue Water Council in Michigan, possibilities within the Explorer program are limited only by the availability of professionals willing to share their time and knowledge. "If a young person is interested in learning about a particular career as an Explorer, I'll try to find someone in that field willing to serve as the post advisor." Occasionally, he'll work in reverse order, finding young people to work with businesspeople interested in establishing a post.

To date, Explorer posts exist in more than 100 career fields nationwide, most of them within public service related fields such as law enforcement, firefighting, emergency rescue service, hospital aides, marine patrol, and conservation. There is even a post which provides teens with the opportunity to learn and work with the U.S. Customs Department.

The Law Enforcement Explorer Post in rural Sanilac County, Michigan, which coordinates activities through the county sheriff department and the local state police post, is just one example of how both sides benefit.

"They are a great help," says Sheriff Virgil Strickler. "In the past six years, calls to our department have risen from 3,000 to 9,000 annually, yet due to economic problems beyond our control, we've had to cut our road patrol from nineteen to fourteen officers. Our Explorers help in a number of ways, from updating inmate records and serving as turnkeys in the jail to managing the front desk and handling dispatches. Without their help, I'd be forced to pull even more officers off road patrol, and I don't have enough money in my budget to pay for extra civilian help."

Sanilac Explorers also spend many summer hours traveling the county on official duty, verifying dog licenses, issuing citations for noncompliance, and making follow-up visits.

Because of the Explorers, the department is also able to staff civic projects that otherwise would have been dropped due to lack of funding or people power. For example, during the county 4-H fair, Explorers staff a free fingerprint identification booth, and in 1989, several Explorers helped the sheriff posse, a horse-mounted adult volunteer unit, with traffic control and gate security.

Advanced training for Law Enforcement Explorers is a mix of classroom study, observing officers on duty, and performing selected tasks under direct supervision. Strict safety guidelines require them to experience the more dangerous side of law enforcement only through simulated situations.

"For obvious reasons, we can't expose Explorers to potentially dangerous situations," explains Detective Greg Ferriby, the Sanilac post advisor since it began four years ago. "We spend a lot of time having the kids react to dangerous situations through simulation. They've learned to search a person for a weapon using the 'stop-and-frisk' method. They've made simulated arrests of dangerous criminals. They've collected evidence and practiced securing a crime scene. Plus, they've learned how to interrogate a suspect and transport a prisoner."

Such intense training often provides unexpected benefits. Explorer Sue Lindsay says it has helped her define which areas of law enforcement she'd most like to pursue. "I realize now I don't really want to be involved with the more violent aspects of being a cop. I knew I'd be scared, only I didn't know how much until I got into the Explorers. We just role play the parts, but Detective Ferriby tries to make the situation as real as possible. You've got to prepare for the worst that can happen. I decided I prefer to work with people in more controlled settings. But, I also discovered that I still want to be in some branch of law enforcement, maybe as a parole officer or counselor."

For Tricia Prowse, the exposure to potential danger as an Explorer took a back seat to the dangers involved with being a cop for real. "My dad didn't want me to join at all. Even though he's a deputy himself, he has always discouraged me from the profession, mostly, I think, because I'm a girl." However, practical experience through the Explorer program has only reinforced Tricia's desire to pursue an active career in law enforcement.

In addition to basic clerical duties associated with law

enforcement, Sanilac Law Enforcement Explorers get actual work experience in three other areas: patrol officer assistant, dispatcher, and corrections officer assistant.

Explorers consider being a patrol officer assistant and a member of the "Ride-Along" program to be the most interesting aspect of the whole program. It has been supported enthusiastically by the International Association for Chiefs of Police since 1979. However, before accompanying an officer on road patrol, Explorers must complete training, which includes becoming familiar with the geographic area for which the department is responsible, practicing communications and radio procedures, and understanding traffic and patrol functions. They also must fully understand the limits of their involvement. For instance, Explorers cannot assist in criminal interrogations, although at the scene of a traffic accident, they may be asked to call for backup, administer first aid, or direct traffic.

You Can Do It

You must be at least fifteen to participate in the Explorer program, although the minimum age varies according to the type of work you'd like to do. Contact your local Boy Scout council for more information about activities in law enforcement as well as other fields. If you don't know the name of your council, contact your local United Way office or write to the Boy Scout national headquarters: Exploring Division, Boy Scouts of America, 1325 Walnut Hill Lane, Irving, Texas 75038-3096. (214) 580-2000.

TEEN FIREFIGHTER

While the Explorer program provides a very organized way for teens to provide public service help in their communities, some teens, like Christy Osborne of Thorp, Washington, volunteer directly. At age sixteen, Christy joined her local volunteer fire department, which meant attending regular monthly meetings as well as attending ongoing training in first aid and firefighting.

Christy's duties as a volunteer include tending the pumps on any of three trucks and serving as a backup person on the hoses. Because of her age, adult volunteers insisted that she not enter a structure fire such as a house, barn, or other building. "But that doesn't mean I didn't get close," explains Christy. "I've come home more than once with singed hair and eyebrows! I've fought house fires from the outside, and barn fires, as well as sagebrush fires and a small forest fire. A house fire is the most depressing as you see people's possessions destroyed by flames, smoke, and water."

As a firefighter, Christy has helped fight a variety of what she calls freeway fires. These include cigarette started grass fires, burning cars, and loaded eighteen wheelers.

She never thought that her job as a volunteer firefighter would be easy, yet it was not exactly what she expected either. "To hear the big siren go off in the middle of the night, fight the darkness and sleepiness as you dress as fast as you can, then tear off running to the station gets your mind racing, and praying—praying that no one's hurt and that no one will be. It's scary. It's work, too. Hard work. But it's worth every bit of the time I've spent with it. It's given me confidence."

You Can Do It

Christy's experience as a firefighter may be unusual. Except through established programs like Exploring, most young people would probably not be accepted as firefighting volunteers at their local fire department. Christy is lucky to live in a small community. She also had the support of her father, who was already a volunteer for the department. However, there are other related opportunities you may wish to pursue. For instance, you might be allowed to help wash equipment and fire trucks or help keep the station and surrounding grounds clean. You might also want to help raise money to buy new equipment or act as a station tour guide for younger students. Don't be afraid to talk things over with the person in charge at your local fire department.

SMART MOVES

By the time he entered high school, John Bramlett had been playing basketball at the North Little Rock, Arkansas Boys Club for four years. The staff there had gotten to know him, and selected him that year for a anti-drug program called Smart Moves.

Through Smart Moves, John and other boys got training on the prevention of drug abuse, alcohol abuse, and teen pregnancies. The Boys Club hoped that these boys would grow to be role models for other club members.

Now, four years later, John still plays basketball and comes down to the club. But there is a great deal more to his involvement. He is one of the peer leaders, an admired older member that the young kids can look up to. John explains, "A lot of kids are going to try to adopt something that they see in me. So I try to be a role model."

For three years, John has taken additional booster classes at the Boys Club on preventing alcohol abuse, drug abuse, and pregnancy. He knows their effect, and he's now in a position to help teach the Smart Moves classes to other kids. "I lead discussions with the younger kids and help when we act out situations," John explains. John also tutors younger kids with their school work two nights a week.

John is there to have fun with the boys, too. He plays games with them and helps mediate the occasional fight. John doesn't have to talk much about the dangers of using drugs or alcohol. Kids at the Boys Club can learn by watching him that it's not necessary to use drugs and/or alcohol in order to feel good about yourself. He says, "Whether I'm helping them one-on-one or playing pool with a group, I think I'm helping. And it makes me feel so good inside. As far as doing something for others, I think I'm accomplishing something."

You Can Do It

John is part of a nationwide Boys Club program called "Smart Moves/Smart Leaders." Call your local Boys or Girls

Club if you'd like to be a part of the program.

If you'd like to do something similar on your own or through your own club, that's possible, too. Just get involved in helping younger kids, perhaps with a tutoring or sports project. They'll look up to you. Show them by your example that drinking and drugs are the wrong way to go.

READING PARTNERS

Every day at four o'clock, thirteen-year-old Anjanette Mozie arrives at her local community center for Reading Partners. Usually a younger child bounces up to her with a book. "Let's read this one," the child will say to Anjanette.

Soon, Anjanette and her "reading partner" have found seats and begun the book. Anjanette doesn't ask her young partners to read. "I just start reading to them, and they just want to join in," says Anjanette. "That's the best way to get them to read themselves."

Anjanette is part of a Charlottesville, Virginia project called Reading Partners. By reading one on one with younger children every day, older children help their partners' reading skills.

Anjanette doesn't even mind kids who want to read the same book every day. "If they read the same book over and over, it's easier for them. They begin to know certain parts."

Participants in the program win awards such as tickets to college women's basketball games or two hours of free bowling. Anjanette and three others won a top prize of a dinner at Pizza Hut.

Anjanette has invented her own addition to the program. After noticing that some of the books used by Reading Partners contained plays, she started her own play reading group. Many afternoons, she now asks, "Who would like to read a play today?" Kids draw up chairs to form a circle. They choose parts and the play begins. Even beginning readers relax and have fun. They know Anjanette will help them if they get stuck on a word.

Reading Partners help each other improve their reading skills. (Used by permission of Susan Sweet.)

You Can Do It

Find out if there is a reading program in your area. Your school may know if a program like Reading Partners is offered through the Boys Club or Girls Club, the YWCA or YMCA, or some other community group. If a program like this doesn't exist where you live, you may be able to start one.

OTHER COMMUNITY PROJECTS

Every youth organization encourages member participation in a variety of community service projects. Ray Jurczyk, program coordinator for the Boys and Girls Clubs of Southeastern Michigan, reports that their projects range from traditional activities like neighborhood cleanup campaigns to more unusual ideas such as the special information fair for "latch-key" children organized by the Redford Township Keystone Service club. The fair featured nine different booths staffed by various professionals, including the telephone company, fire and police departments, and social service agencies. Another group, with members as young as eight, holds an annual Valentine's Day dance and Christmas party where mentally retarded persons from the neighborhood are invited to attend.

Other organizations have started community gardens in vacant lots or helped to raise funds for new playground equipment. Some groups have worked with their local police department to make identification kits for children. Kits include a copy of the child's fingerprints, a current photograph, and an information sheet listing such things as age, weight and height, eye color, and special identifying marks such as moles or scars from injuries.

Other activities that can be done individually or with others include compiling home inventories with pictures and descriptions of family possessions. Young people might also want to compile family histories by interviewing relatives and researching ancestors.

The possibilities are truly unlimited. The following listings include the national offices of many youth organizations. Others are listed under other section categories. If you can't locate a club in your community, contact the national office for help in finding or starting one. Even if you already belong to a youth group, you might want to contact others to see if there is a way to coordinate projects or share resource materials.

Lend a Hand, by Sara Gilbert, offers additional information on programs and contacts, plus includes suggestions for starting your own community project. Check your library for a copy, or call toll free (800) 843-9389; in New Jersey call (201) 227-7200.

Youth View, is a newspaper published eleven times a year which provides information about children and youth and frequently highlights volunteer activities. Although its target audience is families living in Georgia, many of its features are of interest to families living throughout the U.S. A one year subscription is $12. For further information, a sample copy, or a subscription, write: *Youth View*, 1401 West Paces Ferry Road, Suite A-217, Atlanta, GA 30327, or call: (404) 231-0562.

Directory of American Youth Organizations, by Judith B. Erikson, is available from Free Spirit Publishing, 123 North Third Street, Suite 716, Minneapolis, MN 55401, (613) 338-2068.

FOR MORE INFORMATION

Anchor Clubs
Pilot Club International
Pilot Club International Bldg.
P.O. Box 4844
Macon, GA 31213   (912) 743-7403

Boys Clubs of America
771 First Avenue
New York, NY 10017   (212) 351-5900

Boy Scouts of America
1325 Walnut Hill Lane
Irving, TX 75038-3096   (214) 580-2000

Camp Fire, Inc.
4601 Madison Avenue
Kansas City, MO 64112-1278   (816) 756-1950

4-H Youth Development
Extension Service
U.S. Dept. of Agriculture
Washington, DC 20250   (202) 447-5853

Future Farmers of America
National FFA Center
5632 Mt. Vernon Hwy./P.O. Box 15160
Alexandria, VA 22309   (703) 360-3600

Girl Guards
Salvation Army
120 W. 14th Street
New York, NY 10011   (212) 337-7200

Girls Clubs of America
205 Lexington Avenue
New York, NY 10016   (212) 689-3700

Girl Scouts of America
830 Third Avenue
New York, NY 10022   (212) 940-7500

Interact
Rotary International
1560 Sherman Avenue
1 Rotary Center
Evanston, IL 60201   (312) 866-3294

Junior Achievement
45 Club House Drive
Colorado Springs, CO 80906   (303) 540-8000

Junior Deputy Sheriffs' League
National Sheriffs' Association
1250 Connecticut Avenue
Suite 320
Washington, DC 20036   (202) 872-0422

Junior Guardian Angels (see listing page 88)

Junior Optimist Clubs/Octagon Clubs
Optimist International
4494 Lindell Blvd.
St. Louis, MO 63108   (314) 371-6000

Keep America Beautiful (see listing page 116)

Key Club International
Kiwanis International
3636 Woodview Trace
Indianapolis, IN 46268   (317) 875-8755

Keyette International
Ki-Wives International
1421 Kalmia Road NW
Washington, DC 20012   (202) 726-4619

Leo Club Program
Lions Club International
300 22nd Street
Oakbrook, IL 60570   (312) 571-5466

Lutheran Youth Fellowship
1333 S. Kirkwood Road
St. Louis, MO 63122   (314) 965-9000

Naval Sea Cadet Corps
Naval Sea Cadet Corps Headquarters
2300 Wilson Blvd.
Arlington, VA 22201   (703) 243-6910

National Assistance League
5627 Fernwood Avenue
Los Angeles, CA 90028   (213) 469-5897

**National Federation of Catholic Youth
    Ministry** (Formerly CYO)
3900-A Hairwood Road NE
Washington, DC 20017   (202) 636-3825

National Junior Horticultural Association
441 E. Pine Street
Fremont, MI 49412   (616) 924-5237

NCJW Junior Council
National Council of Jewish Women
15 E. 26th Street
New York, NY 10010 (212) 532-1740

Pioneer Clubs
Pioneer Ministries, Inc.
P.O. Box 788
27 W. 130 St. Charles Road
Wheaton, IL 60189-0788 (312) 293-1600

Pirchei Agudath Israel
Agudath Israel of America
84 William Street, 11th Floor
New York, NY 10038 (212) 797-9000

YMCA of the USA
101 N. Wacker Drive
Chicago, IL 60606 (312) 977-0031

Young Marines of the Marine Corps League, Inc.
3523 Lana Lane
Sterling Heights, MI 48077 (313) 939-8996

YWCA
726 Broadway
New York, NY 10003 (212) 614-2700

6.

Health and Hunger

TEENS OFFER AIDS EDUCATION

A group of young teens at the Pontiac Youth Center in Indiana felt kids their age need to know more about AIDS, so they took matters into their own hands and did something about it.

Twenty members of the center organized the Minority AIDS Project for the purpose of performing educational skits and offering tips on how to avoid AIDS. Formed in January of 1989, the group received one year grant funding from the Fort Wayne Youth As Resources board. They also received matching funds from the AIDS Task Force.

During the year, students met weekly at the youth center to write and practice skits, draw posters, and prepare their presentations. MAP Coordinator Helen Frazier says, "I encouraged the members to go right out and mix and mingle, and to stick to their topic. They did a great job and were very well received."

The program attracted exceptional media coverage. Two MAP members appeared on a panel for a local telecast which sought teen reactions to the AIDS epidemic and polled them for ideas on good education strategies. The show preceded the national telecast of *The Ryan White Story*, which depicts a young boy stricken with AIDS.

The Minority AIDS project also appeared in the national broadcast of *America in the Age of AIDS*, a one hour PBS special. The show focused on Fort Wayne, Indiana to show how one city is dealing with the AIDS crisis.

Volunteers for the Minority Aids Project relax after a presentation. (Used by permission of Helen Frazier.)

You Can Do It

If you are interested in coordinating a similar project on AIDS or another health-related topic, contact Helen Frazier, c/o AIDS Task Force, 1012 E. Wells, Fort Wayne, IN 46869, (219) 744-3695.

CAMP FANTASTIC

It takes about twenty-four hours for new teen counselors at Camp Fantastic in Harmony Hollow, Virginia, to stop noticing the physical differences between themselves and their campers. At Camp Fantastic, all of the campers have cancer and suffer from it in varying degrees. But what the counselors soon begin to notice is how much the campers enjoy life.

"These kids' views are really different," commented one teen. "They live day to day. They believe there's no sense in worrying about what's ahead. It may sound funny, but they enjoy life more than we do. They really live it."

While the teen volunteers are there to show campers how to do the things traditionally done at camp, like swimming, crafts, and horseback riding, they often discover that campers are teaching them, too, about important things like tolerance, acceptance, self-reliance, and perseverance.

"They don't give up easily—ever," says Jim Hutchinson, now a five-year veteran of the program. "The camp's permanent staff and the people from the National Institute of Health gave us detailed instructions on what to do for the kids, but ninety-nine percent of the time the kids do for themselves. Even the little ones know when to take their medicine or how to put on an artificial limb."

More importantly, campers teach their teen counselors an appreciation for life. "They made the idea of suicide repulsive," says Jim. "We hear so much today about the epidemic of teenage suicide. It seems to me that the kids who kill themselves have so much to live for. Yet these kids have cancer and still live life to the fullest. They don't want to let go of it. They don't want to waste a minute.

"Driving too fast or drinking a few beers and then cruising around on a Saturday night—anything that might put my life at risk—now seems like such a dumb thing to do. But more than that, the thought of doing those things seems disloyal to the kids from Camp Fantastic. It's like I'd be betraying their trust. They showed us that life is too precious to waste."

Before any camp camaraderie develops there is a big hurdle that each teen staffer must clear: *Nerves.* These aren't ordinary campers they are dealing with. They have very real medical problems. Participation in a good training program helps staff settle a few internal butterflies, yet it can't completely banish the worry volunteers have about how they personally will react, and interact, with campers. Some campers don't seem sick at all, but others look very ill.

"My first day there, I couldn't handle it," recalls Andrea. "I was scared to be with the kids, afraid I'd say something wrong. I didn't know how to act."

"I wasn't ready for it either," adds Jim. "I was so nervous when the bus with the kids pulled up. We had learned about the types of cancer they had at an orientation session, but it was all just words until I saw the kids. Some had lost all their hair from chemotherapy. Some were on crutches because they'd lost a leg. I found myself staring, and then I'd feel guilty about it."

Fortunately, the initial shock begins to fade quickly as everyone turns their attention from cancer to camp. A few worries and doubts keep some butterflies fluttering, but most soon take off. The teens are the ones who have had all the camp training, yet it's the campers who know how to get down to business. And by the end of camp week, butterfly flutters are barely remembered.

"I thought the week at Camp Fantastic would be something I'd have to struggle through, that I'd get to the end and say, 'Thank God that's over with!'" recalls Jim. "But it wasn't like that. It wasn't a depressing place. We spent a week celebrating life. I wanted to stay."

Camp Fantastic is only one of the programs sponsored by Special Love, a nonprofit corporation cofounded by

Teen volunteers serve as camp counselors to cancer patients at Camp Fantastic. (Used by permission of John Dooley.)

John Dooley, director of the Northern Virginia 4-H Center where camp is held, and the Baker family of Winchester, Virginia, who lost a daughter to cancer and wanted to use their own experience to help other families with sick children. The Bakers came up with the idea for a summer camp that would allow children to spend a week away from their ordinary routine of anxious parents, doctors, and limited activity. At the same time, Mr. Dooley was looking for a growth experience program for his 4-H teen counselors.

Camp Fantastic has provided a unique way that allows teens not only to put their leadership skills to work but also to give them the challenge of a lifetime. Since Special Love began, nearly a hundred teens have participated as volunteer counselors. They work under the supervision of an adult volunteer staff which includes doctors and nurses.

Many teen counselors have changed dramatically as a result of their Camp Fantastic experience. Many rethink their former career plans, changing them completely or adjusting them so they can maintain some link to the experiences they've had at camp. Some plan careers in community service or as doctors and researchers.

In addition to its summer camp for kids with cancer, Special Love now sponsors a variety of programs year round, including a camp for the elderly held at Christmas time, a camp for kids with diabetes, and one of the few camps in the country for hemophiliacs. And each program depends on the enthusiastic service of teen volunteers.

You Can Do It

Many hospitals and national health-related organizations sponsor camping programs. Young volunteers are often recruited through youth organizations such as 4-H or Scouts. If there is a camp near your home, you may be able to volunteer without leaving your own area. But if there is no program nearby, you may want to consider an away-from-home camp experience. Search for sources by contacting various medical facilities in your area. Check with staff at various youth organizations, or write to one or more national disease groups such as the American Cancer Society, to see what they sponsor and whether young people can volunteer.

In addition to counseling duties, volunteers are often needed as kitchen staff or ground maintenance crews. Many other types of youth camps also need volunteers. For additional leads, check with school counselors or local church leaders.

MOCK DISASTERS AND EMERGENCY RESCUE SERVICES

"Catherine Hayward lay motionless as rescue workers raced toward her and others involved in an airplane crash Wednesday at Detroit Metropolitan Airport."

That's how a September 21, 1989, *Detroit News* article began. Accompanying photos showed a pair of bloodied young passengers cradling each other on the lawn and dozens of emergency medical technicians hovering over people on stretchers. Even though the story was about volunteers participating in a mock disaster drill, it sent shivers up many readers' spines.

Catherine Hayward, seventeen, was just one of many students to volunteer as victims for the drill. In all, 156 volunteers from throughout the community and 1,500 rescue workers participated. While organizers plotted and evaluated the most efficient ways to respond, "victims" moaned and groaned their way through a wide variety of cuts, bumps, breaks, and bruises while waiting for "treatment" from emergency medical and rescue teams. As the first rescue worker arrived to tend her, Catherine reported on cue, "I'm okay, but my fingers tingle."

Mock disasters are played out regularly around the country. They simulate a number of both manmade and natural calamities from hurricanes and floods to toxic waste leaks and food poisoning. Though the drills themselves are taken very seriously, the overall tone for volunteers, especially those playing victims, is normally one of light hearted community spirit. After all, it's hard to get

These injuries are just temporary! Teens help emergency preparedness by taking part in disaster drills. (Photo by David C. Coates. Used by permission of Detroit News.*)*

worried about being swept away in a tornado when the sky is a robin's egg blue and you can smell coffee brewing in the refreshment tent.

However, for Catherine as well as other volunteers, this particular disaster drill seemed almost too realistic. That was understandable. It was the first drill in the county since Northwest Airlines Flight 255 crashed just after take-off on August 16, 1987, killing 156 people.

"It scared me," said Catherine. "All I could think was, 'What if this was really happening to me?'"

Among the people who frequently help out in both mock and real disasters are amateur radio operators, known as HAM operators. They are sometimes the only communication in and out of a disaster area.

Rosalie White, Education Coordinator for the American Radio Relay League says, "During Hurricane Hugo there were an awful lot of power and telephone lines down. And a lot of the communications that came out of the area were strictly through amateur radio.

"A lot of practice for emergencies is done all the time. It's not always for a hurricane or earthquake. HAMs often track bikers or runners during marathons."

There are no minimum age requirements to become a HAM operator. It depends entirely on a person's passing the Federal Communication (FCC) test. According to Ms. White, "We have members ranging in age from six to over sixty, and I know of several instances, personally, where a young HAM operator relayed a distress call."

People with computers and modems are adding a new link in emergency services. For instance, soon after the October 1989 earthquake shattered the San Francisco Bay area, CompuServe created several on-line assistance programs including Earthquake Forum; Earthquake News, a special Executive News clipping file; a special reports section in On-line Today; and information about the Bay area WATS line, which served members who did not have local access.

HamNet, a forum dedicated to serving the needs of amateur radio and short-wave (SWL) operators, offered communications assistance by radio, relaying on-line messages to worried families and friends. Others sent electronic mail messages to California-based members, asking about their safety.

CompuServe reports that more than 2,000 messages were exchanged in the Earthquake Forum service during its two-week service span.

You Can Do It

Rescue workers in mock disasters are usually volunteers from organizations such as the Red Cross, as well as professionals from various medical and public service fields. However, "victims" in a mock disaster can be almost anyone. Captain Mark Sparks, Wayne County Emergency Management Director, suggests that young people interested in volunteering as "victims" in a future mock disaster drill contact someone at their local Red Cross chapter or emergency management department. "Call, or better yet, write a letter," he says. "Tell them that you would like to participate.

"Guidelines vary in different communities and also within different participating groups in the same community. However, even if elementary age children are not welcome at a full-scale mock disaster, smaller 'disasters' can sometimes be planned between a school or youth group and a public service or health agency."

AMERICAN RED CROSS

The American Red Cross is probably the best known of all the voluntary, emergency service organizations. Its youth involvement program, first established as the Junior Red Cross in 1917, is among the oldest in existence. Over the years, millions of young people have participated in many community, national, and international service projects.

"We depend on young people a lot for our programs," says ARC Youth Associate Susan Walter. "There are too many needs in our country and around the world for us not to involve youth in service."

The Red Cross estimates as many as two million elementary and middle school youth have helped on individual projects such as collecting food or clothing for the needy. These programs are usually coordinated directly with schools and community groups through a local Red Cross chapter. Young people are also quick to respond to disasters whether they occur near them or far away.

To meet emergency needs, the Red Cross often requests donations of cash rather than supplies. Donors can specify that their contributions be used to assist a particular cause, like earthquake or hurricane victims. However, many people, including students, prefer to give to the general Disaster Relief fund, which allows the money to be used where it is needed most and in a way that is most effective.

Learning basic first aid and CPR (cardio-pulmonary resuscitation) is an obvious additional benefit to being involved with the Red Cross. Lives have been saved by even very young children who have been exposed to first aid training. One three-year-old is credited with saving his mother's life when he followed one of the first rules of first aid—get help—and called 911 when he saw his mother choking. Other Red Cross youth volunteers help in hospitals, "adopt" a grandparent in a nursing home, become part of the Red Cross "clown corps," or train to be part of a community disaster action team. But another program attracting more and more young volunteers is the student blood-donor program.

One high school senior says that donating blood in school is one sure way of skipping class without getting in trouble. But, through personal experience, he realizes the importance of the contribution he's making and admits it makes him feel good to volunteer.

"Blood shortages are a real problem in many areas, including mine. Several years ago my mom hemorrhaged real bad and needed a large blood transfusion. She's got an odd blood type, B negative, and the hospital had trouble finding enough of the right kind."

For him, giving blood has become part of a family tradition. "My grandpa has taken time out from farming to donate blood every few months for years. So far he's given close to eight gallons. Neither my mom or dad can donate blood because of medical problems, but I'm healthy, so why not? At school, a couple of kids passed out the first time they did it. But they volunteered again during the next blood drive. My younger sister plans to donate blood, too, as soon as she's old enough."

You Can Do It

The American Red Cross has an enormous collection of health, emergency service, youth participation, and volunteer program guides available. Some are offered free through the Red Cross; others have fees. Contact either your local Red Cross chapter or the national headquarters office for complete information about available resources.

HELPING THE HUNGRY

Sherry Shadden has learned that harvesting crops is not easy. As she says, "I still have nightmares about the squash I picked."

Getting up at dawn, having breakfast, and being in the fields by seven a.m. is not most teenagers' idea of a fun week. After all, summer vacation is supposed to be just that—a vacation.

Still, Harvest of Hope has never had any problems finding enough willing participants to take part in their week long retreats to help the hungry. The program has its base in the fact that, every year, tons of perfectly good food are wasted simply because portions of crops are left to rot in the fields. As good as modern technology is, farm equipment that can pick every piece of produce has not been invented. The only way to get that part of the crop is for human hands to pick it up. Farmers do not have the capacity to provide this labor, so this food was always wasted until teenage volunteers stepped in to save the day. Organized by the Society of St. Andrew, a Methodist-affiliated group, these kids work in week-long retreats to salvage the food. Usually between forty and fifty kids participate. At the end of the week it is all distributed to food kitchens, soup

Corn gleaned by Harvest of Hope volunteers will help feed the hungry. (Used by permission of Harvest of Hope.)

kitchens, and shelters throughout the country.

Sherry Shadden, a resident of Houston, Texas, has taken part in two Harvest of Hope retreats. One of those was in Sequin, Texas, where the group gleaned squash and zucchini. The physical labor was done in the morning, and in the afternoon classes were held on hunger, its impact, and what can be done to combat it. Group members all become very close, because they've worked so hard together. "By the end of the week I felt I had known most of those kids since birth. We all had a common goal, and even though our political and social views differed, we banded together as one," Sherry says. Indeed they did, since at the end of the week they donated over 10,000 pounds of produce to the area food bank.

You Can Do It

Harvest of Hope retreats are located in many states, including Texas, Louisiana, Virginia, South Carolina, New York, Maryland, Minnesota, and Pennsylvania. Harvest of Hope is for senior high school students. Another program, called the Glean Team, has been developed for junior high students. Weekend and day gleaning programs, in which kids can take part with their families, are also held. To find out more, contact the Society of St. Andrew, P.O. Box 329, State Rt. 615, Big Island, VA 24526, (800) 333-4597.

FOR MORE INFORMATION

American Cancer Society
261 Madison Avenue (212) 599-3600
New York, NY 10016 (800) ACS-2345

America Red Cross
Programs & Services Department
17th & D Streets NW
Washington, DC 20006 (202) 639-3039

Harvest of Hope
Society of St. Andrew
P.O. Box 329
State Route 615
Big Island, VA 24526 (800) 333-4597

Special Olympics International
1350 New York Avenue NW
Suite 500
Washington, DC 20005 (202) 628-3630

Muscular Dystrophy Association
810 7th Avenue
New York, NY 10019 (212) 586-0808

National Multiple Sclerosis Society
205 E. 42nd Street (212) 986-3240
New York, NY 10017 (800) 227-3166

7.

Kids Helping Kids: Peer Support Groups

INVENT AMERICA!

INVENT AMERICA! encourages kids to invent creative solutions to everyday problems or irritations that they or their friends or family face regularly. Since the program's founding in 1987, millions of students from kindergarten through eighth grade have designed and demonstrated a wide range of inventions.

Steve Prater, from Indianapolis, Indiana, was both a local and regional winner in 1989 with an invention he calls a *handwriting stabilizer*. He designed it for his school friend Sheryl Stratton, whose cerebral palsy had made it impossible for her to write during the previous seven years.

The invention is a rubber glove, weighted with a bit of plaster, that Sheryl wears over her hand. It has a pencil holder on the side and a roller from a deodorant bottle embedded in the plaster which allows Sheryl to glide her hand along the paper. A foam rubber device has grooves for her to grip, which also helps her stabilize her fingers as she writes.

Like many of the world's most used inventions, such as lead pencils and Post-It notes, Steve's invention was relatively easy and inexpensive to make. But first he had to come up with a workable solution. It took him about two weeks of hard thinking and working out various designs on paper. The next step was to assemble it. That took about two days. The total cost of the handwriting stabilizer was about five dollars.

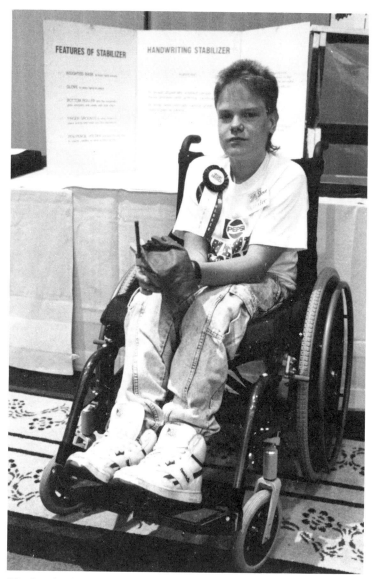

The handwriting stabilizer, Steve Prater's own prize-winning invention, helps those who have difficulty writing. (Used by permission of INVENT AMERICA!)

Sheryl field tested the stabilizer by writing her name and taking a test at school. "I'm pretty happy with it," she reports.

An invention that helps the disabled seems a fitting problem to solve for a student like Steve. He has spina bifida. "His legs don't work," says Maurine Marchani, a teacher at Stonybrook Junior High School. "Everything else does, however, especially his mind." Not to be content with a single prototype, Steve is now designing a similar glove for his mother, who has severe arthritis.

You Can Do It

Kevin O'Brien, Program Vice President for INVENT AMERICA! shares this advice for young inventors: "Find something that bothers you every day, something you'd like to see work better, or a special problem you think needs to be addressed. Identify the problem and then work towards a solution."

Mr. O'Brien suggests to young inventors that they "remember that a good invention is one that solves the problem most simply, efficiently, and economically. Don't look for ways to make it complicated—look for ways to streamline it. A good invention can be something very simple in design and execution. Above all, it should be easy to use, practical, and serve a useful purpose."

INVENT AMERICA! is a nonprofit endeavor, supported by corporations and groups such as K-mart, Lego, Mastercard International, Pepsi-Cola, Polaroid, and the Kiwanis International. Each year, INVENT AMERICA! sponsors an annual student invention competition for students in grades kindergarten through eighth, which provides national recognition and more than $600,000 in awards for students, their schools, and teachers. You may obtain an INVENT AMERICA! Starter Kit which includes all the necessary information on the program and handbooks and contest entry forms by writing to: INVENT AMERICA!, Starter Kit, 510 King Street, Suite 420, Alexandria, VA 22314. (703) 684-1836. The Starter Kit materials are free, but please include $2.75 for postage and handling.

My book for kids with cansur

A Child's Autobiography of Hope

Dr. Gaes Offis For Kids With Cansur

A portion of the proceeds f

Hospitals are fun about the first 2 or 3 days. Then they get boring so bring coloring books and toys for when cartoons arent on. If you're grown up bring cards.

GET WELL

Then I had toomers so I take medasin th It's called keymothar is medasin that dr in your arm called in your back call

Ivs

My Book for Kids with Cansur *uses Jason's own handwriting and his brothers' illustrations. (Copyright 1987 by Jason Gaes. Published by Melius & Peterson Publishing Corporation.)*

PEER SUPPORT FOR KIDS WITH CANCER

When Jason Gaes was six years old, doctors discovered that a rare form of cancer called Burkitt's lymphoma was growing rapidly inside him. No one expected him to live long enough to celebrate his seventh birthday. However, Jason pulled through and fully recovered after two years of operations and many painful treatments, including radiation and chemotherapy.

During that time, one thing that bothered Jason a lot was that all the children's books about kids with cancer had sad endings. Everyone always died. He decided to write a book about his own experiences—a book that showed that kids who get cancer don't always die. Originally, Jason planned to give the book to his grandfather as a present. But when his parents read his book, they asked Jason for permission to share it with others.

"I didn't think an eight-year-old could have anything profound to say," says Jason's mother, Cissy. "But unbeknownst to me, he had dealt with some very complex issues. It was the story of what happened to him in his own words."

Mrs. Gaes decided to ask Jason if photocopies of the book could be used as invitations to a "cancer party" that he had requested be held once his treatments were finished. "He was real hesitant at first," says Mrs. Gaes. "But I talked him into it."

The invitations went out to family and friends and many of the doctors and nurses that had worked with Jason. An invitation was also sent to some staff members from the American Cancer Society, who were so impressed with Jason's book that they wanted permission to make copies to hand out to other children with cancer. "It was the most we could have hoped for, that someone else could read it," says Mrs. Gaes.

On the day of the party, a television news reporter, curious about why anyone would throw a "cancer party," came to do an interview. They told her about Jason's battle with cancer and how he came to write the book. Later that night, a publisher in South Dakota heard about Jason and his book on the evening news. He called and asked to see a copy. The next thing the Gaes's knew, Jason had a book contract.

Jason's book, *My Book for Kids With Cansur*, was published as a regular book with a hardcover, but just as Jason had handwritten it. Jason's two brothers, Tim and Adam, drew the illustrations.

Soon Jason's message of hope was being shared in more ways than anyone ever imagined. Jason was interviewed by newspaper and magazine reporters and asked to appear on many television shows. Since then, he has also talked with many students at school assemblies and community events about what it's like having cancer. Jason even starred in an HBO award-winning documentary called, "You Don't Have to Die."

Jason, now twelve, doesn't talk about his celebrity status much, even though his book has also been published in Canada, Japan, and West Germany. He still gets lots of requests to speak at schools, fundraisers, and health conferences. He says that sometimes he gets bored telling the same story over and over. "But then you realize that not everyone in the world hears you the first time, and you know you're helping a lot of kids."

What he doesn't mind discussing as much are all the phone calls and letters he has received from kids with cancer. So far he's gotten about 10,000, mainly because he put his home phone number and address in the book, so kids with cancer can call or write to him if they get scared.

"I remember this one girl," Jason says. "Her name was Angela. She was five years old and she called the night before she was going to have an operation. And I talked to her. She wanted to know what would happen if she woke up during the operation. So I told her that there is a doctor at the top of your head making sure you don't wake up, so everything would be okay except when you wake up you might be a little sore. After the operation, she called up again and said, 'Thank you a lot.'"

Jason thinks it would have been nice if there had been a kid like him to talk to when he had cancer, especially before he knew he was going to be okay. "When a kid has cancer he says, 'Oh, poor me. I'm probably going to die because I've never heard of anyone that's lived from this stuff.' And when you hear about me—I had one of the worst kinds, a kind that barely any of them could treat — and learn that I beat mine . . . well, then maybe some kid with leukemia would get a little better positive feeling." In addition to helping other kids with cancer, Jason says writing the book helped him deal with it, too. But he warns that sharing such a personal experience isn't always easy. "You know, if you're going to write a book or talk about what happened, you've got to go back and think of everything. And sometimes it's really hard to go back and write the things that used to happen to you like waking up at night really scared and having those dreams. That kind of hurts."

A portion of the proceeds from the sale of his book go to the American Cancer Society. It is distributed by Melius Publishing, Inc., 515 Citizens Building, Aberdeen, SD 57401. Or call (800) 882-5171 for more information.

Kids with cancer can write to Jason at: 1109 Omaha Avenue, Worthington, MN 56187.

You Can Do It

Writing a book about one of your own experiences is a good way to help other kids who may be in the same situation. By sharing your experiences you let them know they are not alone, and show them how you made your way through a tough time. Your experience does not need to be as serious as that which Jason went through for it to help others, though. Your book does not have to have such national exposure, either. Even if it helps only one or two other kids it is still worth it!

BANANA SPLITS

Being a kid can be tough. And some times are rougher than others, especially when someone you love suddenly dies, your parents get divorced or remarried, or something else equally upsetting happens, and you can't do anything about it.

Occasionally, students at Wood Road Elementary School in Ballston Spa, New York, go through rough times like that too. However, they have a program called Banana Splits which helps them deal with their problems. It began in the early 1980s as an informal rap session at which students met to discuss personal problems. It is now a recognized peer counseling program involving about 200,000 kindergarten through twelfth grade students each year across the country. Members meet with other members of approximately the same age and grade level.

"Students want to know that they're not alone, that others around them are experiencing similar feelings and difficulties, and that they can survive the dramatic changes taking place in their lives," says Elizabeth McGonagle, who developed the program.

Members of Banana Splits peer counseling group gather for a party. (Used by permission of Elizabeth McGonagle.)

"Splits," as members call each other, meet either once or twice a month, and participation is voluntary, although members must have their parents' permission to attend. Splits agree that anything said at a meeting is strictly confidential. It is *not* to be repeated as a part of playground gossip.

A highlight activity for the Banana Splits of the entire Ballston Spa School District is an annual end-of-the-year party where pizza and, of course, banana splits are served.

You Can Do It

A 100-page manual detailing the Banana Splits program is available for $15.50 from Elizabeth McGonagle, Wood Road Elementary School, Ballston Spa Central Schools, Ballston Spa, NY 12020. (518) 885-5361.

YOUTH AS RESOURCES

The Youth As Resources program encourages teens to work in partnership with area adults and businesses. It emphasizes delivery of community services by youth as opposed to delivery of service by adults to youth. Teens participate in developing and governing a wide range of projects as well as coordinating with other young people to help carry them out.

Under a grant from the Lilly Endowment, Inc., The National Crime Prevention Council (NCPC) in Washington, DC, is responsible for the general organization and administration of YAR programs including training, reporting, and oversight of various locally-based YAR boards.

Each local YAR program is guided by a board of directors consisting of local leaders (including young people or teens) in community service, business, education, justice, youth affairs, social and employment services, and communications.

The board funds projects in which young people work in their community and contribute to its vitality and improvement. Grants for projects range from $100 to $5,000, with most falling in the $1,500 to $3,000 range. Local boards and YAR staff are active in encouraging applications for grants; screening, selecting and monitoring grantees; and training.

In 1988, four communities were selected by NCPC to serve as demonstration sites. They were charged with the job of implementing YAR's goals and ideals within their communities. Three of the programs were located in Indiana; the fourth was in Boston, which was also the site of the first project.

You Can Do It

Any nonprofit organization can host a Youth As Resources project. Grants have been sought by a variety of community organizations from city probation departments to 4-H Junior Leaders.

Terry Modglin, Director of Youth Programs for NCPC, reports that Youth As Resources programs are expected to spring up in other cities as interest spreads. Anyone, including teens, interested in information about Youth As Resources can contact the YAR Program Director, NCPC, 733 15th Street NW, Washington, DC 20005, (202) 466-6272.

FOR MORE INFORMATION

Alateen
Al-Anon Family Group Headquarters, Inc.
P.O. Box 862, Midtown Station
New York, NY 10018-0862   (212) 302-7240
Fellowship of young Al-Anon members, mostly teens, whose lives have been affected by someone else's drinking.

American Children Exercising
  Simultaneously (ACES)
Valley View School
Montgomery Avenue
Montville, NJ 07045

Purpose of ACES is to call attention to the importance of physical education. In 1989, more than 230,000 students nationwide participated in the program through a one day symbolic gesture of fitness and unity. For more information about the program and future dates, send SASE to Lenny Saunders, Project ACES at the above address.

Drug Hotline (800) 662-HELP

Does not give counseling help by phone but can refer people to help groups in their area. Can also send informational brochures regarding support services.

Friends
Lutheran Social Services of North Dakota
Box 389
1325 S. 11th Street
Fargo, ND 58107 (701) 235-7341

Network of people who have been through various stressful situations and who are available to help others when needed. Persons having a particular emotional problem are matched with a volunteer who has had a similar experience.

Good Bears of the World
Box 8236
Honolulu, HI 96815 (808) 946-2844

Promoters and collectors of teddy bears who distribute them to children in hospitals (also to seniors in institutions) as a symbol of love and affection. Publishes newsletter.

Junior Deputy Sheriffs' League
National Sheriffs' Association
1450 Duke Street
Alexandria, VA 22314 (703) 836-7827

Members are encouraged to use positive pressure to help keep peers out of trouble. The group also acquaints young people with local government and provides training in emergency preparedness.

Junior Guardian Angels
c/o Karen Skrivseth
8836 Birchwood Lane
Bloomington, MN 55436   (612) 944-1492

Open to kids age ten through their sixteenth birth-day. (At sixteen, they may join a senior Guardian Angels club.) Junior Angels do not go on patrol. However, they meet regularly, learn martial arts training, and participate in a variety of community service projects. Most important, Junior Angels provide each other with positive peer support by encouraging each other to stay in school, obey the law, and adhere to the Guardian Angel code of conduct at all times. Minneapolis was the first area to sponsor a Junior Angel program and will share information on how to start a Junior Angel program on request. If possible, enclose two first class stamps to cover postage costs.

Just Say No Clubs
Just Say No Foundation
1777 N. California Blvd.
Suite 200
Walnut Creek, CA 94596   (415) 939-6666

Clubs may stand alone, or the program may be incorporated as part of an existing youth, school, or other community group. Members can attend peer counseling training sessions to prepare them for giving presentations to peers and younger students.

"I Care" Program
Student Activities Director
Mumford High School
Detroit, MI 17525   (313) 270-0430

Students are encouraged to participate in week long campaign designed to promote self-esteem among students. Program goals are threefold: learn to care about yourself, your education, and others around you. Program also encourages kids to take the "I Care" message with them throughout the year, and to serve as positive role models for younger students. Free program packet available for those interested in establishing a similar program. SASE is appreciated.

National Association for Visually Handicapped
305 E. 24th Street
New York, NY 10010   (212) 889-3141

Publishes newsletter, *In Focus*, for visually handicapped kids.

Students Against Driving Drunk
P.O. Box 800
Marlboro, MA 01752   (617) 481-3568

SADD is an international citizen activist organization whose goals are to: help students eliminate their number one killer–drinking and driving; to encourage students to use positive peer pressure to save lives threatened by drinking and driving and drug abuse; to conduct parent and community awareness programs that promote the care-giving triangle of home, school, and community; to deal with these issues in an affirmative fashion; and to encourage students not to drink or use illegal drugs. Also sponsors the Student Athletes Detest Drugs program.

Local SADD chapters can be established in high schools, middle schools, and colleges throughout the nation at relatively little cost. General information and guidelines available free on request.

Students to Offset Peer Pressure
STOPP Consulting Services
P.O. Box 103
Hudson, NH 03051-0103   (603) 889-8163

Members are high school aged young people dedicated to promoting a drug free environment by providing alternatives to drugs. Also sponsors Junior STOPP program for grades five to eight, and STOPP-A-TEER Clubs for preschool through grade five.

Teens As Resources Against Drugs
National Crime Prevention Council
1700 K Street NW, Second Floor
Washington, DC 20006   (202) 466-6272

Encourages teens to use positive pressure to stop peers from using drugs.

Twelve Together Program
Metropolitan Youth Foundation
13105 W. 7 Mile Road
Detroit, MI 48235   (313) 864-1400

Project offers counseling and peer group support to high school freshmen in groups of twelve, and is aimed at keeping fellow students from dropping out of high school. Also encourages members to serve as good examples and mentors for younger students. For more information contact Gwen Moore, c/o the above address.

Youth To Youth
CompDrug
700 Bryden Road
Columbus, OH 43215   (614) 224-4506

Sponsors annual summer training conference for teams of adults and youth working in drug and alcohol prevention programs. Drug education materials available.

Additional resources:

Rainbows For All Children offers curriculum materials and training for peer-support programs geared to elementary and high school students and parents for use by schools, social agencies, and churches. For more information, write 1111 Tower Road, Schaumburg, IL 60173, (312) 310-1880.

The Pittsburgh Center for Stepfamilies, has school based counseling programs for children and parents. Write the center at 4815 Liberty Avenue, Suite 422, Pittsburgh, PA 15224, (412) 362-7837.

8.

Working with Animals

ANIMALS AND FRIENDS VISIT SHUT-INS

In Sebastapol, California, local 4-H members have taken various farm pets, such as chickens, ducks, pigs, and sheep, with them when they visit area nursing homes. One member even brought along a miniature horse.

The visits were started by fourteen-year-old Becca Hall. Although the visits are appreciated by almost all residents, Becca says that contact with 4-H volunteers and their animals seems to be especially beneficial for elderly patients afflicted with severe memory loss.

"The animal visits help some of the forgetful patients remember handling animals in the past," she explains. "And then the patients remember more about what they did and who they were, which increases their self-esteem."

You Can Do It

This activity requires prior planning, preferably in conjunction with an organized youth group experienced in animal handling, such as various 4-H or local pet clubs. Before visiting, volunteers should meet with staff members at potential visitation sites to discuss a number of matters, including liability resulting from possible accidents or injuries, the types of animals that may be brought in, and who will be responsible for cleaning up animals' "accidents." Ideally, young volunteers should offer to handle any clean up needed.

A 4-H member brings a baby pig to visit with a nursing home resident. (Used by permission of Jeremy Hall.)

Volunteers helping disabled riders have as much fun as the riders themselves. (Photo by Laura Pretorius. Used by permission of Kluge Children's Rehabilitation Center.)

Visiting animals need to be tame enough to tolerate handling by strangers and should not spook too easily in unusual surroundings. It might be wise to organize a trial visit first, perhaps during a regular club meeting.

This type of visitation project can also be adapted for schools, group homes for mentally retarded individuals, or senior citizen residences.

THERAPEUTIC HORSEBACK RIDING

When Stephanie Logan saw the newspaper advertisement for volunteers to help disabled children with horseback riding, she called right away.

"I was only twelve then," says Stephanie, "and I was worried that I would be too young to volunteer for the program." The Kluge Children's Rehabilitation Center for Therapeutic Riding was happy to have an enthusiastic volunteer like Stephanie, and she has been helping out weekly ever since.

Three to six children come to ride on the afternoon when Stephanie volunteers. Some of the kids are mentally retarded. Others are physically handicapped by conditions like cerebral palsy. Riding helps these kids exercise weak muscles and gain self confidence. On horses they move with a freedom that they do not have on the ground.

"They are so happy to be there and so excited. It's really neat to see them," says Stephanie.

Children often remember a special horse and request it week after week. Sometimes the children are so excited that Stephanie and the other volunteers have to calm them down a little before they can ride. Then the program's director helps each child onto a horse.

Two or three volunteers help with each horse and child. The volunteer having the most experience with horses is given the job of leading the horse. The other two volunteers walk or run on either side of the rider. They are the side walkers. Stephanie prefers to be a side walker, since it gives her a chance to talk to the children and frees her of the responsibility of controlling the horse. "All the kids are different," she says. "For some, we need to hold onto their belts. Others just need a steady hand on their leg. Some need only one side walker."

Before the children begin riding each week, they do some exercises on horseback. Volunteers ask them to touch the ponies ears or reach down and touch their own foot.

It is the children themselves who give the horses their commands. Once they have permission from the director, they are the ones to tell the horses to "Walk on" or "Trot." "The kids learn that they are really riding those horses, not just being led around the ring," says Stephanie.

As the children ride, the side walkers remind them about safe riding technique. Stephanie explains, "We always tell them to look between the pony's ears. We remind them to hold on to the reins and keep their heels down." Some children get so excited about riding that they forget easily.

"It's really neat to see the kids so happy. That's why I've been doing it for three years," says Stephanie. "It's really fun."

You Can Do It

Although Stephanie had riding experience before signing up as a volunteer, it is not a requirement for this kind of program. However, most programs do require that their volunteers be at least fourteen years old. The riding center where Stephanie volunteers, the Kluge Children's Rehabilitation Center for Therapeutic Riding in Charlottesville, Virginia, is part of a national group called the North American Riding for the Handicapped Association. If you would like to learn more about volunteering, contact their national office at P.O. Box 33150, Denver, Colorado, 80233. Their directory lists more than 400 therapeutic riding centers across the country. Each needs volunteer help and offers an orientation program for new volunteers.

Remember, this kind of activity requires special training and special horses. Riding for the handicapped should take place only under professionally supervised conditions.

LEADER DOGS FOR THE BLIND

Would you like to raise a puppy and feel that your playing with that puppy would some day help a blind person? Then perhaps you should get in touch with Leader Dogs for the Blind or one of several other organizations that trains dogs to lead blind people. These groups encourage volunteers to participate in puppy raising programs.

"Right now we have 200 puppies placed with foster families throughout the Midwest area," says Julie Mullikin of the Leader Dogs. "Some of these families have children and some don't."

All the puppies come from Leader Dogs' purebred breeding program and are either Labrador Retrievers, Golden Retrievers, or German Shepherds.

Foster families are responsible for a puppy from the time it is seven or eight weeks old until it is returned at the end of twelve to fifteen months. All puppies must be kept as inside pets and taught basic house manners, as well as general commands such as sit, come, and stay. Ms. Mullikin stresses that puppies must be exposed to as many situations as possible.

"We need the dog to be extremely socialized," says Ms. Mullikin. "If it's your own dog, you may only have it around your own family and never take it out. But to be a Leader Dog candidate, it must be well behaved on a leash."

Although formal obedience training is not required (a manual is supplied to help families follow program guidelines), foster families are encouraged to take the puppy on car rides and walking around town. Ms. Mullikin says that having another animal in the house is okay, especially if it's another dog. "As a matter of fact, it actually benefits puppies, because when they come back for training, they will obviously be around other dogs."

Ms. Mullikin also stresses that interested families need to remember that all puppies are owned by Leader Dogs and must be returned to the training center at the end of the fostercare period. Sometimes it is very hard for people the give up the dogs. However, whenever a Leader Dog completes final training, the original foster family receives a picture of the dog and its new owner.

You Can Do It

Leader Dogs encourages young people interested in the puppy raising program to join through a 4-H puppy-raising group in their area. If no club exists, or if a family prefers to participate on its own, contact Leader Dogs directly for an application and program policy guidelines: Leader Dogs for the Blind, 1039 S. Rochester Road, Rochester, MI 48063. (313) 651-9011. Visitors are welcome to tour the facility by appointment.

There are a variety of programs similar to Leader Dogs for the Blind operated around the county. To find one in your area, Julie Mullikin suggests contacting your local humane society or area school for the blind.

CANINE COMPANIONS FOR INDEPENDENCE

The puppy raising program through Canine Companions for Independence is very similar to that sponsored by Leader Dogs for the Blind. However, CCI dogs are trained to assist people with disabilities other than blindness. Through specialized commands, Canine Companion dogs become the physical extensions of their disabled owners by pulling wheelchairs, signaling important sounds, pressing elevator buttons, turning on light switches, and generally being ready and able to perform a variety of basic tasks designed to help the physically challenged be more independent. You can spot a CCI dog by the bright yellow cape it often wears in public.

There are five regional CCI training centers located throughout the United States. In addition to puppy raisers, volunteers can also help at the training centers. Their duties may include general office or public relations work or keying data into the computer. Volunteers also give talks about CCI to groups and clubs, and work in information booths at fairs and special events. Experienced volunteers may also assist puppy class instructors during Saturday classes or help in the kennel area grooming, bathing, exercising, watering, and scooping. Volunteer assistant instructors help with classes for disabled students.

You Can Do It

Suzanne McKellar, a volunteer at the Southwest Regional Center, says CCI doesn't have a policy regarding minimum age for volunteers because of the variety of things which could be done. "If a child was really interested and appeared responsible, they might be allowed to volunteer. They could help with the newsletter or stuffing envelopes," she says. "They certainly wouldn't be turned away." Information about CCI's puppy-raising program as well as other volunteer opportunities is available from any CCI regional center.

Northwest Regional Training Center
1215 Sebastopol Road
Santa Rosa, CA 95407   (707) 579-1985 Voice/TDD

Southwest Regional Training Center
P.O. Box 8247
Rancho Santa Fe, CA 92067 (619) 756-1012 Voice/TDD

North Central Regional Training Center
6901 Harrisburg Pike
Orient, OH 43146   (614) 871-2554 Voice/TDD

Northeast Regional Training Center
P.O. Box 205   (516) 694-6938
Farmingdale, NY 11735-0205   Voice /TDD

Southeast Regional Office
P.O. Box 547511   (407) 682-2535
Orlando, FL 32854-7511   Voice/TDD

HELPING HANDS

Since 1979, tiny capuchin monkeys have been trained to help quadriplegics perform countless small tasks during the course of the day. A quadriplegic is a person who is

Many kids help to raise puppies for Leader Dogs for the Blind. (Used by permission of Leader Dogs for the Blind.)

unable to move his or her arms and legs. The disabled person communicates his or her needs to the monkey by aiming a small, wheelchair mounted laser light pointer at the object he wants the monkey to manipulate. The laser beam, plus a voice command, indicates what the monkey is to do with the object. When the monkey has completed a task, the quadriplegic owner rewards it with both verbal praise and a treat from the reward dispenser mounted on his or her wheelchair.

In this way, a disabled person can direct a monkey to perform tasks such as placing a book on a reading stand or getting a drink from the refrigerator. The monkey can also be trained to transfer prepared food from a refrigerator to a microwave and position food containers for feeding. It can select cassette tapes, compact discs, or VCR cassettes, and put them into the right playing unit. Monkeys will also come when called and return to their cage on command, locking the door behind them.

Monkeys used for this unique program are bred in a special colony located at Walt Disney World in Orlando, Florida. However, baby monkeys are raised in foster homes in a program similar to the puppy raisers described earlier.

The program is open to interested families throughout the United States. Ms. Zazula stresses that raising a baby monkey requires a tremendous amount of time and effort.

One restriction of the Helping Hands program is that foster families cannot include children under the age of ten. Staff worker Judith Zazula explains that the combined demands of young children and baby monkeys can be overwhelming. "Baby monkeys require the same care as infants, including bottle feeding and diaper changing."

Foster families receive babies when they are between six and eight weeks old and care for them until they are three or four years old. Then the monkeys are returned to the training center in Boston.

High school teens in the Boston area can also volunteer directly at the training center. Ms. Zazula says, "Teens are always needed to help with light office work, cage cleaning, watering plants, cage cleaning, vacuuming, cage cleaning, cage cleaning, and cage cleaning. Of course, they also get the chance to be around the monkeys."

You Can Do It

Young people interested in raising a monkey for Helping Hands must have the complete support of their families. In many ways, it will be like having a new baby brother or sister in the house. You might even get jealous of the attention the new baby gets! And unlike puppies, infant monkeys can not be left alone, so you'll need the help of a parent or adult friend to "monkey sit" any time you go away.

Interested families can obtain an application and detailed information about the program by contacting: Helping Hands, Simian Aides for the Disabled, Inc., 1505 Commonwealth Avenue, Boston, MA 02135 (617) 787-4419.

OTHER ANIMAL PROJECTS

Many of the most interesting and exciting activities involving animals involve foster care programs. However, they require a strong, long-term commitment on the part of the volunteer and his or her family. If you have trouble remembering to care for a pet your family already owns, the novelty of being a foster parent to a dog or monkey will quickly wear off. And if you've never owned a house pet before, you're bound to be surprised and overwhelmed at the round-the-clock work involved. Consider, too, how you will feel when it comes time to give the animal back so it can begin its specialized training program.

Learn about pet care by completing some short-term projects first. At school, offer to take turns caring for classroom critters like hamsters, white mice, snakes, or fish. Offer to walk a friend's dog on a regular basis or consider adopting or house-sitting the neighbors' pet while they go on vacation.

Most humane society shelters rely on volunteers to help clean cages, feed and exercise animals, and assist with general office chores. Some veterinarian clinics may also welcome volunteer help.

Interested in wildlife? Then contact the public relations department at your local zoo, nature park, or animal preserve. Sometimes you'll be encouraged to join a nonprofit organization that provides support to the facility through fundraisers or community awareness projects. Various groups also train volunteers to act as tour guides or to provide other support services for their local facility. Check to see if young people are welcome to participate in your area.

If circumstances don't allow you to participate directly in animal programs, you might want to help by becoming a member of a national or local wildlife society.

FOR MORE INFORMATION

American Society for the Prevention of Cruelty To Animals
Education Department
441 E. 92nd Street
New York, NY 10128   (212) 876-7700
Publishes resource materials promoting humane treatment of animals. Some are especially suited to young people.

Children's Action for Animals
American Humane Education Society
350 S. Huntington Avenue
Boston, MA 02130

Supports club or classroom-based programs that help young people in understanding animal life. Catalog available.

Earthwatch — (see listing page 145)

4-H Youth Development — (see listing page 60)

Heifer Project International
International Livestock Center
Route #2
Perryville, AR 72126   (501) 889-5124
Offers work camps for volunteers in ninth grade and up at the livestock center. Young people from the

U.S. and abroad learn about livestock and raise heifers for developing countries. Write to the volunteer coordinator for brochure and application.

Intersea Research
P.O. Box 1667
Friday Harbor, WA 98250   (206) 378-5980

Open to families interested in combining either seven or eleven day sailing experience while helping to conduct whale research. Travel costs involved. Location sites are off the Alaskan and Hawaiian coasts.

Junior American Horse Protection Association
1038-31st Street NW
P.O. Box 3586
Washington, DC 20007

Conducts education programs for children and adults interested in the protection of both wild and domestic horses.

National Audubon Society
National Education Office
RR#1 Box 171
Sharon, CT 06069   (203) 364-0520

Audubon Expedition Institutes are available for young people twelve to fifteen; additional expedition programs open to youth sixteen and over. Has special materials developed for Native American youth. Local affiliates offer many opportunities for participation by young people. Various resource materials available.

National Zoological Park
Smithsonian Institute
3001 Connecticut Avenue
Washington, DC 20008   (202) 381-7335

Information resources cover history, nature, science, medicine and zoo management.

Paws for Cause
Ears for the Deaf, Inc.
1235 100th Street SE
Byron Center, MI 49315   (616) 698-0688 TDD/Voice

Sponsors a puppy raising program. Adult dogs are trained to help the deaf "hear" by alerting owners to noises such as a baby crying, telephone or doorbell ringing, smoke alarm, intruder, etc. Some dogs also trained as service companions for the physically disabled. Families with children are welcome as puppy raisers. Also occasionally uses volunteers directly at training facility. Contact Candye Sapp, Associate Director for more information.

World Wide Pet Lover's Society
P.O. Box 1166
Hurst, TX 76053

Nonprofit pen pal society for pet lovers. Has 10,000 members; 5,000 are children in kindergarten through eighth grades. There are no fees, charges, or dues. Young people wishing to become pen pals need to send two first-class postage stamps. In return they are sent three or four names of other pen pals with whom to start correspondence.

9.

Protecting the Environment

TROUT UNLIMITED

Trout Unlimited is a national nonprofit organization dedicated to the enhancement, preservation, and restoration of the nation's cold water fishery resources. Many members are active in a variety of environmental programs such as clearing waterways of both manmade and natural debris, as well as conservation projects such as positioning deflectors to protect trees along stream banks from being undercut and erecting specially designed log or rock dams.

In 1989, for the first time, a special program just for kids was developed that encourages participation in Trout Unlimited's environmental and conservation projects. Known as the Fishing for 4-H club, it is co-sponsored by the Arlington County Cooperative Extension and the Northern Virginia Chapter of Trout Unlimited. Tobin Smith, who is an active member of both sponsoring groups, founded the club and serves as advisor. Club members can be between the ages of eight and nineteen.

Like adult members of Trout Unlimited, Fishing for 4-H members want to learn more about fishing as a sport. However, they are also eager to participate in environmental projects. Their first project was to help with the annual spring clean out of Four Mile Run in March of 1990. That stream is of special interest to club members as it runs directly through Arlington and is stocked early each spring with trout, another of Trout Unlimited's projects.

Fourteen-year-old Joey Manson, current club president, explains that without those projects, there would be no fish in the stream to catch. "Plus," he adds, "we want to help teach people that you don't need to keep all the fish that you catch. Fishing should be done as a sport. You can catch a fish for fun and then throw it back so someone else can try to catch it. If everybody kept all the fish they caught just to hang on the wall, pretty soon there wouldn't be any fish left to catch." Joey adds that people who want fish to eat should buy it from stores that get it from places that raise fish specially for food.

Charles and Phillip Carpenter are nine-year-old twins and among the club's youngest members. Since joining the club they feel they are more aware of the how many times people do things to harm the environment without really thinking. "Once I saw a police officer," explains Charles, "and it looked like he was telling these two men to dump their beer in the stream because they weren't supposed to have any in the park. I think that was wrong because the beer could kill things [in the water]. The police officer could have just taken it away."

Phillip agrees. He adds, "I don't think anyone is too young to learn how to fish or help keep the environment clean."

You Can Do It

According to Tobin Smith, one of the best things about the Fishing for 4-H program is that it could be easily duplicated in almost any area of the country. Since it is a new program, he suggests contacting him first at the Northern Virginia Chapter of Trout Unlimited for information on starting a fishing club co-sponsored by a Trout Unlimited chapter near you. The address is: Tobin Smith, Youth Coordinator, Northern Virginia Chapter, Trout Unlimited, 1753 Mercer Road, Haymarket, VA 22069.

Your local Cooperative Extension office can also provide background information about conservation and possible ongoing programs.

Cleanup is more fun when everyone helps. (Photo by Cathryn Berger Kaye. Used by permission of the Constitutional Rights Foundation.)

Los Angeles youth help their community by painting out graffiti. (Photo by Cathryn Berger Kaye. Used by permission of the Constitutional Rights Foundation.)

NEIGHBORHOOD IMPROVEMENT

Eighteen-year-old Pedro Reyes gets things done. And he believes that other teens can too. This is his advice for other kids who want to do something for their community: "If they see something wrong, they can do something about it. Just get out there and do it."

Pedro, a high school senior from Los Angeles, is a member of Belmont High School's Youth Community Service Club. But you get the feeling from talking to Pedro that he'd be out working to improve his community whether he was a club member or not. And he believes one person can influence another. "Say I want to clean up trash from a neighborhood. I can talk to one person, and if he decides to do it, he tells someone. It's like a little chain. That person tells someone, and that person tells someone. . .."

A lot of Pedro's activities do begin in his club. The club meets every Friday during lunch. Anyone can suggest a project for the club to work on. The club has cleaned up neighborhoods, taught blind children, painted out graffiti, planted trees, and more.

Pedro has become their tree expert. He completed a special class to become a Citizen Forester, even though he was the only high school student in a class full of adults. To combat the greenhouse effect, he organized his club to plant trees at the high school and at a day care center. Pedro studied which kind of trees would be best for each site. The trees had to be able to withstand drought and have deep roots that wouldn't break through the concrete. For the day care center, Pedro chose trees that would provide good shade for the children on hot days.

Pedro calls his club a melting pot. Club members include Latinos like Pedro as well as students with Chinese, Japanese, Cambodian, and Philippine heritage. They all work together when a project comes up.

"People really support us. We get a lot of paint and stuff donated. When we're out in a neighborhood working, people will come out and give us water and sodas. They'll start working, too. Gang members may come by and talk negative, but we ignore them."

There was a time when Pedro wasn't interested in community service or in school. "I almost got kicked out of school in junior high. I was hanging out with bad kids. But little by little I started to turn around. I decided that the purpose of my life was more than that. When I started high school I got a fresh start."

Pedro was shy when he first started his community service work. It was hard for him to approach people for help or to speak in front of a group. Because Pedro was determined to make a difference, he learned how to get things done. He figured out how to get permission from the Los Angeles School District to plant trees. He found out that there was paint available at city hall for community projects. Recently, Pedro received a national award for his volunteer work. With new confidence, he spoke to the thousands of people who were in the audience at the awards ceremony. He even appeared on the *Today* show.

Now Pedro is looking forward to college, a term in the Peace Corps, and a career in counseling. "There is no community service club at the college that I'm going to. I think I'm going to have to start one," say Pedro.

You Can Do It

Pedro Reyes's volunteer club is sponsored by School Youth Service, a part of the Constitutional Rights Foundation, 601 South Kingsley Drive, Los Angeles, CA 90005. The organization helps clubs in twenty-four Los Angeles high schools. It also publishes a newsletter called *Network*, which is full of ideas for volunteer projects. The newsletter is available to people in any part of the country.

So even if you don't live in Los Angeles, you can get ideas from the newsletter. And everyone can learn something from Pedro, who has shown that people who care can make a difference.

YELLOWSTONE RECOVERY CORPS

Six teens from the Bronx, New York, organized through the New York Park Council's Urban Conservation Corps, were among the hundreds of volunteers who spent a week or more living in Yellowstone National Park during the summer of 1989. Their assignment: to help clean out, rebuild, and improve areas of the park devastated by fierce forest fires in 1988. For many, this was their first time camping out, and they needed to learn not only their rigorous volunteer duties but how to set up camp and survive in the wilderness.

But by the time they returned home, the whole crew was talking about hanging bear lines (stringing cables up in trees on which to store food out of reach of bears), handling the mules and horses that carried supplies, and living with other crew members in the back country.

Carolyn Angiolillo, program director of the New York Urban Conservation Corps, reports that for many of her corps members, it was their first time on a plane, first time out of the city, and the first time they were exposed to a natural wonder such as Yellowstone. "It was hard, scary, and they felt uncomfortable many times," she says. "But they had the opportunity to work, to see different types of people, and to learn that the world is bigger than the one they know. It was an eye-opening and very positive experience for city kids."

Not all Yellowstone Recovery Corps members were from the city. In all, members participated through seventeen different youth corps groups that stretched geographically across the United States. The program itself was organized by the National Park Service, the Student Conservation Association (SCA), and the National Association of Service and Conservation Corps (NASSC). Most of the SCA recruits were high school volunteers. Volunteers spent a minimum of two weeks living and working in Yellowstone, with most staying for at least a month.

Crews first arrived in mid-June and worked through

mid-October. Each crew was composed of six corps members plus a supervisor. Some crews were assigned to the back country, where they cleared burned trail areas that were too dangerous for hikers and built bridges over streams. They also cleaned out fallen trees and helped put in place erosion control structures on the scars left by bulldozers used to fight the fire.

The main job of the front country crews was resupplying crews in the back country with food and equipment. They often hiked distances of six to eight miles carrying fifty-pound loads. Sometimes front country crews, traveling by helicopter, were sent out for a week to the back country to reseed trees in remote areas where bulldozers had plowed through to create firebreaks.

Among the services provided to participants through NASSC was an education program about the natural and human history of Yellowstone. A library of books about the park as well as a dictionary and thesaurus was given to every crew supervisor. Each crew kept a journal with individual members being required to write something each day.

"These kids felt as though they were participating in a national effort, and they seemed very proud to be a part of it," according to Yellowstone Project Director and NASCC staff member, Carl Menconi. "Corps members regularly report that the Yellowstone program is a life changing experience."

Other people are also proud of the dedicated effort of the 1989 Yellowstone Recovery Corps. The project was deemed so successful that the National Park Service planned to continue the project at least through 1991.

You Can Do It

Young people interested in more information about programs such as the Yellowstone Recovery Corps or others sponsored by the Student Conservation Association (SCA) and the National Association of Service and Conservation Corps (NASSC) can contact the national office of Youth Service America for information and referrals. YSA is also the best resource to contact for community based conservation programs. High school students interested in summer work camp programs in remote wilderness regions may contact SCA directly for program information.

RECYCLING PROJECTS

Everywhere across the country, there is an upsurge of interest in recycling. To save our natural resources and reduce pollution, people are sorting used glass bottles by color, squashing aluminum cans, and bundling newspapers. In some places, recycling is mandatory, and recyclable items are picked up at the curbside of people's homes.

But in other areas, the decision to recycle depends on the individual, and his or her concern for the environment. This is where you can have a role. The easier it is for people to recycle, the more likely they are to do it. Find out how you or your group can help—by staffing a recycling center, helping with pick ups, or spreading the word about the importance of community recycling.

If your group decides to begin a recycling program, be sure to find a company willing to accept the material that you collect. You may even make a little money, especially by collecting aluminum. But be careful. Right now, the technology for recycling and reusing newspaper still needs some improvement. This means that is some areas it is hard to find a company willing to accept old newspapers because they cannot find paper companies willing to buy them.

Also, be sure to do a good job of sorting the glass. At least one community has had the sad experience of having its collected material rejected. The glass was not sorted well and had paper and trash mixed in.

You Can Do It

To find out what's already being done in your community, check with local civic officials at your city or town hall, your local Chamber of Commerce, the department of public works, or the supervisor at the local landfill. In addition, local environmental action groups usually know

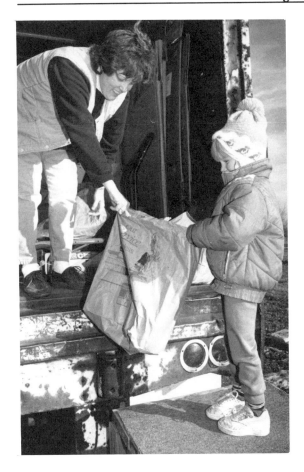

Volunteers everywhere can help with recycling. (Used by permission of Ardyce Czuchna-Curl)

what's going on in the recycling area. The education division of your state Department of Natural Resources can also help you locate recycling centers, as well as being an excellent resource for additional information.

A special recycling guide, *Why Waste a Second Chance?*, for residents of small towns is available for $10.00 plus $1.50 for postage and handling from the National Association of Towns and Townships, 1522 K Street NW, Suite 730, Washington, DC 20005.

FOR MORE INFORMATION

Appalachian Mountain Club Trails Program
P.O. Box 298
Gorham, NH 03581   (603) 466-2721
Projects are located within national parks. Minimum age is sixteen; younger participants sometimes allowed when accompanied by parents. Some project costs involved. Write for complete information.

Archaeological Institute of America
Box 1901 Kenmore Station
Boston, MA 02215   (617) 353-9361
Does not sponsor projects itself, but does publish an annual edition of archaeological field opportunities.

American Hiking Society
P.O. Box 86
North Scituate, MA 02060

Volunteers must furnish camping gear and arrange for transportation to project site. Project locations include Alaska, Wyoming, and Virgin Islands. Must be experienced backpacker. Youth under eighteen must have parental consent; under sixteen must be accompanied by an adult.

Army Corps of Engineers
Omaha District
215 N. 17th Street
Omaha, NE 68102

Plans and builds projects for flood control, navigation, and water conservation; during emergencies aids local authorities. Also manages recreation at a number of lakes. Available information includes history, nature, recreation, and science.

Bureau of Land Management
Office of Public Affairs
Department of the Interior
Washington, DC 20240

Offers information on the management of over 400 million acres of national resource lands mostly in ten western states and Alaska. Topics include: camping, hunting, fishing, hiking, rock hunting and off-road vehicle use. Also information on primitive, historic, natural, or scenic areas.

Bureau of Reclamation
Department of the Interior
Public Affairs Service Center
Denver Federal Center, Bldg. 67
Denver, CO 80225

The bureau is the primary water resource development agency of the federal government operating in the seventeen western states. Two programs include environmental education and public involvement.

Civil Service International/USA
c/o Innisfree
Rt #2 Box 506
Crozet, VA 22932   (800) 823-1826

Project locations within the United States are open to those sixteen and over.

Ducks Unlimited, Inc.
One Waterfowl Way
Long Grove, IL 60047   (312) 438-4300

Information regarding the preservation and management of wetlands which attract waterfowl.

Earthwatch—(see listing on page 145)

Fish and Wildlife Service
Room 3240, Interior Bldg.
Washington, DC 20240

Many local and regional offices throughout the U.S. Available resources include information on youth conservation corps as well as a variety of material on nature, wildlife oriented recreation, and ecological science.

Keep America Beautiful
99 Park Avenue
New York, NY 10016   (212) 682-4564

Sponsors various projects aimed at environmental improvement. Resource materials available on conservation service projects and proper waste handling.

Friends Weekend Work Camps
1515 Cherry Street
Philadelphia, PA 19102   (215) 241-7236

Participants from outside area are encouraged to apply. Open to volunteers fifteen and older.

Greenpeace, USA
1436 V Street, NW
Washington, DC 20009   (202) 462-1177

Service locations and opportunities vary. Apply for information and application forms. Also has need for volunteers to work at home office in Washington, DC.

Izaak Walton League of America
1701 N. Fort Meyer Drive, Suite 1100
Arlington, VA 22209   (703) 528-1818

Sponsors Save Our Streams, a citizen action program which welcomes young volunteers. Also publishes other materials related to the protection and wise use of natural resources.

National Energy Foundation
5160 Wiley Post Way, Suite 200
Salt Lake City, UT 84116   (801) 539-1406

Sponsors variety of youth programs to promote awareness of energy-related issues and concerns. Has both people and print resources available. Catalog available upon request.

National Park Service
Office of Communications
Room 3043, Interior Bldg.
Washington, DC 20240

NPS is a conservation organization set up to protect natural and historical areas. Many regional offices located throughout the U.S.

National Wildlife Federation
1412 16th Street NW
Washington, DC 20036-2266   (800) 843-1714

Subscribers to *Ranger Rick* magazine automatically become members of Ranger Rick's Nature Club. Local clubs are organized in various communities. Also publishes a wide variety of conservation education and nature study at relatively low cost. Catalog available upon request.

Sierra Club Outings
Service Trips
739 Polk Street
San Francisco, CA 94109   (415) 776-2211

Volunteers must be in good physical condition and able to backpack at high altitudes. Projects include cleaning debris along rivers and trails. Write for further information and age/experience restrictions.

Soil Conservation Service
Department of Agriculture
Box 2890
Washington, DC 20013

Publishes a variety of general and technical publications on most aspects of SCS programs on soil and water conservation. Information available to help citizens and groups plan conservation projects.

Student Conservation Association, Inc.
High School Work Groups
P.O. Box 550
Charlestown, NH 03603   (603) 826-5206

Each year approximately forty-five projects are planned which involve over 350 high school students
from all across the country in three to five week long
coeducational outdoor environmental work groups
comprised of six to twelve students and one or two
adult supervisors. Projects are coordinated through
several government and private land management
agencies, including the U.S. Forest Service and state
park areas. Among the jobs volunteers perform are:
trail construction and maintenance, timber stand improvement, wildlife habitat improvement, building
and repairing fences, construction of structures such
as shelters, privies, and bridges, and archaeological
field survey work. Write to above address to an application and listing for the summer program.

Touch America Program
American Forestry Association
P.O. Box 2000
Washington, DC 20013   (202) 667-3300

Offers programs for young people ages fourteen-
seventeen, including conservation work camps on
public land in conjunction with other groups. Resource materials available.

Trout Unlimited
National Headquarters
501 Church Street, NE
Vienna, VA 22180   (703) 281-1100

U.S. Forest Service
Department of Agriculture
Box 2417
Washington, DC 20013

Offers reference sources and information. Young
people can also contact their own state Department

of Agriculture for the location of their regional Forest Service office.

Youth Service America
1319 F Street NW, Suite 900
Washington, DC 20004   (202) 783-8855

Sponsors a variety of community based environmental and/or and conservation projects in conjunction with local schools, city or state government departments. Through Youth Volunteer Corps of America, YSA targets programs to young people ages thirteen to eighteen from a wide range of cultural and economic backgrounds. Youth Service America also has many other thought-provoking resources, ranging from videotapes to booklets on youth serving the elderly.

Additional Resources

Shopping for a Better World—Resource catalog listing approximately 1300 products for "people who want to be socially-responsible" shoppers. Order from: Council on Economic Priorities, 30 Irving Place, New York NY 10003, (800) 822-6435. Cost is $5.95 which includes shipping.

The Adventure of Adolescence: Middle School Students and Community Service, by Catherine A. Rolzinski—Profiles of middle school community service projects across the country. Order from: Youth Service America, 1319 F Street NW, Suite 900, Washington, DC 20004.

10.

We the People:
Political Awareness

GIVE PEACE A CHANCE

The assignment: Create an invention that would benefit the world. Michelle Alexander, a thirteen-year-old from Fresno, California, took the school assignment seriously. The result, however, has proven extraordinary.

For her assignment, Michelle invented a board game called "Give Peace a Chance." Since creating her game, Michelle has become an ambassador of good will, promoting peace and human rights worldwide.

At the invitation of the United Nations, Michelle met and played "Give Peace a Chance" with the chief peacemaker of the world, the Secretary General of the United Nations, Mr. Javier Perez de Cuellar. She has also played the game with other international diplomats. In the Soviet Union, the Foundation for Social Inventions, run by Komsomolskaya Pravada, has set up a fund in Michelle's name to finance projects for children. Each year she will visit the Soviet Union, where she will serve on a board to help determine the distribution of the funds.

Her game has been used as an exhibit at the UN during the International Conference on Nuclear Disarmament. She has been recommended as a Youth Ambassador for the United Nations Disarmament Conference.

The game has earned two international awards including the Corita Kent Peace Award presented in March 1989. Michelle, herself, has been nominated for many awards including the Reebok Human Rights Award. And Disney/

MGM recently awarded her their Hall of Fame Award for her continued commitment to making the world a safer place for all.

Michelle believes that people need to think about each country's dependence on other countries. Whether she is meeting with other children or world leaders, her message is the same. "What we do for world peace and human rights as kids today matters for us as adults tomorrow." Her game promotes the concept that, "We all win if there is world peace."

To play the game, players choose to become a "country" by selecting one of 170 printed paper flags and slipping it into a flag holder which is used to move about the game board after the roll of the die.

Countries gain or lose peace tokens depending on the directions on the game board, or by having to take a peacemaker or peacebreaker card. In some instances all countries may benefit from the action of another country, or the countries may all lose tokens based on the action of another country. Each of the thirty game board spaces and each of the peacemaker or breaker cards offer thought-provoking concepts about peace.

Michelle's newest creation is her "Peaceful Thoughts" booklet geared for children ages five to twelve. Children have the opportunity to write answers to peace related questions and do word searches and other games.

You Can Do It

The "Give Peace a Chance" game and other peace re-lated products are produced by: Peace Works, Inc., 3812 N. First Street, Fresno, CA 93726, (209) 435-8092. Young people interested in sharing their thoughts on world peace and human rights with Michelle can write to her at the same address.

You may also want to invent a board game of your own. A board game on an important issue such as peace or the environment is a good way to teach people while they're having fun.

CONGRESSIONAL AIDE PROGRAM

Through a "Wider Opportunity Program" sponsored by the Girl Scout Council of the Nation's Capitol, older teens in the Washington, DC area can become volunteer aides to senators and state representatives from around the country. Terms are from one to four weeks during the summer. In addition to working, volunteers have an opportunity to meet many of the nation's political leaders as well as gain valuable firsthand knowledge of the legislative process.

In 1989, Amy Schnirel served as a congressional aide for two representatives, Bob Traxler of Michigan and Jim McCrery of Louisiana. She was surprised to discover that her efforts as a volunteer were really appreciated. There was always mail to open, questionnaires to sort, and filing to do. She was even sent to the Library of Congress to check some facts.

Janine Kushner, who also served as an aide for Representative Traxler, was even asked to draft a response for him in answer to a young girl's letter.

"The Congressional Aide Program is absolutely wonderful," says Congressman Traxler. "I have sponsored young women from this program for the past two years and have been greatly impressed by their ability to participate in everyday professional activities."

The Congressional Aide Program was developed about sixteen years ago and started with just a few girls going into offices. Now approximately 125 weeks worth of service is given by eighty to ninety aides each year in some ninety-five congressional offices.

You Can Do It

Despite the success of this program, René Shackelford, Older Girl Program Specialist for Girl Scouts in the DC area, isn't aware of similar programs elsewhere. However, she feels that they could be done equally well in other areas and by most any youth organization.

"What they would have to do is get support from their

legislative process first to see if there is a need, and to see whether the state legislators want volunteers there," says Ms. Shackelford. "From there you can build the program together."

She urges those interested in pursuing the project to start small and is willing to make her council's program guidelines available to others to use as a model.

If you don't live in your state capital, find out if you can volunteer at nearby city or county government offices.

To receive additional program information contact: Girl Scout Council of the Nation's Capitol, 2233 Wisconsin NW, Washington, DC 20007, (202) 337-4300.

TEEN REPUBLICANS

Howard Hogan of Ridgefield, Connecticut, was fourteen and a freshman in high school when he first began exploring ways to get involved in the political process.

"I wanted to find an after-school activity that would combine my interest in politics and world affairs with my desire to help people," he says.

When he couldn't find an existing organization that met his criteria and embraced his own Republican philosophies, he got a few friends together to found a club on their own. He didn't know that a nationwide young people's Republican club not only did exist, but had been growing steadily for over twenty years. That organization was the National Teen-Age Republicans (TARS).

"We didn't know TARS existed. So, at first, we wrote letters to our Congressmen and the White House. We also got in touch with our local first selectmen (elected city council members) and also our local Republican town committee.

"The Republican town committee though it was a wonderful idea and were very supportive, as were the selectmen. They gave us an advisor who had been on the board of selectmen. All of them were instrumental in helping us get started."

Howard says he even got a letter back from the White House congratulating them and wishing them well.

Included were several pieces of literature related to the Republican Party. Someone at the White House also send his name to the TARS headquarters in Washington, which contacted him almost immediately.

"It was kind of funny," says Howard, "because when we found out about TARS, it seemed to be everything we wanted in a club."

The Ridgefield TARS boasted about six members, all freshmen, their first year in existence. Now, the club has approximately forty members, including students from all four high school years as well as some graduates.

Howard says that he doesn't think he would have been interested in TARS any earlier, even if he had known it existed. "When I was younger, I was just starting to sort out my own political ideas and establishing my identity.

"You see," he says, "I wasn't born a Republican. Both my parents are liberal. My dad's been a Democrat all his life. So being a Republican wasn't something that just came naturally to me. It evolved after a lot of thinking and reading and learning. I don't know if I would have been ready when I was in middle school for this kind of activity."

Ridgefield TARS activities are divided into three areas. The first encompasses political activities which are mostly concentrated from September through November. Members volunteer as workers in a variety of political campaigns, doing whatever the candidates or the local Republican committee asks of them. "This runs the gamut from stuffing envelopes to going door to door, to making posters and putting up signs, to whatever," explains Howard. "We also attend various political rallies and functions."

Their second focus area is to learn and experience the world of politics. Activities might include visiting the state capital or going to local political organization meetings such as Citizens for Peace Through Strength. "We also meet with representatives from other political or service-type organizations," says Howard.

For instance, during the 1988 presidential race, Ridgefield TARS conducted a month-long project to follow the Republican presidential primaries. They sent away for literature from all the campaigns, watched the debates, and

Members of Teen-Age Republicans clean up a local cemetery. (Used by permission of Howard Hogan.)

had discussions. "We even had a little nominating caucus," says Howard. "We had supporters from all the campaigns nominate their candidate in front of us. So members got to practice their public-speaking skills. Then we had a mock poll."

As their third focus, Ridgefield TARS participate in a variety of community service projects. "We got very active with JUST SAY NO day in town. We even donated the symbols that kids put on their t-shirts."

Other projects have included sprucing up the town cemetery just before Memorial Day and placing flags near the tombs of veterans. Every year right before Christmas, Thanksgiving, and Easter, TARS holds a food drive and prepares and delivers food baskets for the needy in town. They coordinate their efforts with other service clubs such as the Lions and Knights of Columbus.

Many of their service activities are projects they have initiated themselves, although other groups frequently ask for their help. Howard says, "We get invitations to help out all the time. And we're always glad to do it. As a matter of fact, we have a standing offer to help senior citizens with things that they can't do for themselves anymore. We've done things like mow lawns or help people move."

Asked if the TARS had ever encountered any problems, Howard responds, "For the most part, the community has been overwhelmingly supportive. Even Democrats and liberals like the fact kids are getting politically active, as I think anyone would. We have a lot of liberal teachers at school, but that only helps us to hone our political views and debating skills."

Howard is not sure how his current involvement with the Republican Party will affect his life later on. He's not sure whether he would ever want to run for an elected office himself. "My political beliefs and my desire to do whatever I can to help will always be with me," he says. "I know that I will always be a strong supporter of the Republican Party. And I know that I'll continue to do whatever I can to forward its goals of individual freedom and prosperity. But I don't know how at this point."

You Can Do It

A wide variety of support materials are available through the National TARS headquarters. These materials include information on campaign techniques, the Republican platform and philosophy, community service ideas, how-to materials and more. Interested youth might also want to contact their state TAR advisor or local Republican committee for help in establishing a local TAR club. Write or call: National TAR Headquarters, Megan Beth Lott, Organizational Director, P.O. Box 1896, Manassas, VA 22110, (703) 368-4214. From the Washington, DC area call: 631-9625.

Currently the Democratic Party does not sponsor a national club for young people. But there is no reason not to start one on your own. Contact your local Democratic Party for assistance.

FOR MORE INFORMATION

Boys State/Boys Nation
American Legion
(Contact state Legion headquarters.)
Model government program for high school juniors, chosen through their schools, to acquaint young people with political processes and the ways in which governments function. Two representatives from each state program are chosen to attend Boys Nation.

Girls State/Girls Nation
American Legion Auxiliary
(Contact state Legion Auxiliary headquarters.)
Model government program for high school juniors, chosen through their schools, to acquaint young people with political processes and in which governments function. Two representatives from each state program are chosen to attend Girls Nation.

Congressional Youth Leadership Council
John Hines, Executive Director
1511 K Street NW, Suite 842
Washington, DC 20005 (202) 638-0008

Junior Optimist–Octagon Clubs
Optimist International
4494 Lindell Blvd.
St. Louis, MO 63108 (314) 371-6000

Civic-service organization for junior high (Jr. Optimist) and high school (Octagon) students. Promotes active interest in good government and civic affairs.

Junior Statesmen of America
Junior Statesmen Foundation
650 Bair Island Road, Suite 201
Redwood City, CA 94063 (415) 366-2700

Organization of high school student leaders interested in politics, government, and current issues. Programs are carried out by students with minimal adult assistance.

National Association for the Advancement of Colored People
Youth and College Division
4805 Mt. Hope Drive
Baltimore, MD 21215-3297 (301) 358-8900, Ext. 9142

Organization seeks to achieve equal rights and the elimination of racial prejudice for all American citizens. Some communities sponsor Junior Councils for young people ages four to twelve.

National Association of Student Councils
1904 Association Drive
Reston, VA 22091 (703) 860-0200

Federation of student councils sponsored by the National Association of Secondary School Principals. Promotes student government. Write c/o Dale D. Hawley, Director of Student Activities.

National Network of Youth Advisory Boards
P.O. Box 402036
Ocean View Br.
Miami Beach, FL 33140   (305) 532-2607
Promotes youth participation in the decision-making process and youth programs in such areas as education, employment, drug and alcohol abuse, recreation, and justice. Provides technical assistance to help community leaders establish youth participation councils or advisory boards.

National Traditionalist Caucus
P.O. Box 971, G.P.O.
New York, NY 10116   (212) 685-4689
Program for junior/senior high students that stresses patriotism, conservative values, anti-Communism, and free enterprise.

Presidential Classroom for Young Americans
441 N. Lee Street
Alexandria, VA 22314   (703) 683-5400
Sponsors programs for high school, graduate and undergraduate students, and teachers that provide an in-depth study of the United States government in Washington. Conducts week long program of seminars for high school students.

Robert F. Kennedy Memorial
917 G Place NW
Washington, DC 20001   (202) 628-1300
Provides opportunities for young people to affect their communities and society at large.

Spartacus Youth Clubs
c/o Spartacus Youth Publications
P.O. Box 3118, Church Street Station
New York, NY 10008   (212) 732-7860
Sponsors the Spartacist League/U.S. for young adults ages fifteen to thirty.

Students for America
3509 Haworth Drive, Suite 200
Raleigh, NC 27609   (919) 782-0213

Teen-Age Republicans
National TAR Headquarters
P.O. Box 1896
Manassas, VA 22110

Young Americans for Freedom
300 I Street NE, Suite 3A
Washington, DC 20002   (202) 547-6631

The oldest and largest bipartisan conservative political youth group for ages up to thirty-nine. Promotes free enterprise, a strong national defense, and traditional Judeo-Christian family values.

Young Democrats of America
c/o Democratic National Committee
430 S. Capitol Street SE
Washington, DC 20003   (202) 863-8000

Primarily for young adults ages eighteen to thirty-six who want to foster the aims of the Democratic Party. Does not currently sponsor a separate youth program. Young people are advised to contact the local or state Democratic Party if they wish to be involved in promoting Democratic platforms, candidates, etc.

Young Socialist Alliance
14 Charles Lane
P.O. Box 1235
New York, NY 10013   (212) 334-1110

Promotes Socialist ideals among students and young workers.

Youth Against War and Fascism
46 West 21st Street
New York, NY 10010   (212) 255-0352

For high school and college students and young workers who oppose war, imperialism, racism, and other forms of discrimination. Also actively supports prison reform.

Youth and Government
YMCA of the USA
101 N. Wacker Drive
Chicago, IL 60606   (312) 977-0031
Program for high school students which stresses that
democracy must be learned by each generation.
Young people participate in model state legislatures
and the Annual Governors' Conference held in
Washington, DC each summer. Top debaters from
each state may participate in the annual Youth Conference on National Affairs.

Additional Resources

Center for Peace and Freedom
214 Massachusetts Avenue NE
Suite 380
Washington, DC 20002

National Center for Public Policy Research
300 Eye Street NE, Suite 3
Washington, DC 20002   (202) 543-1286

Washington Workshops Foundation
3222 N Street NW, Suite 340
Washington, DC 20007   (202) 965-3434

The White House
1600 Pennsylvania Avenue NW
Washington, DC 20500   (202) 456-1414

White House Comment Line   (202) 456-7639

11

Friends around the World

FRIENDSHIP BOX PROGRAM

The Friendship Box Program, sponsored by the American Red Cross Youth Services, is an excellent class, group, or individual activity. Students fill boxes about the size of a small shoe box with health, educational, and recreational items which are then sent on to children in other areas both nationally and abroad.

The boxes that go to other countries may be used by children affected by natural disasters. Boxes with school supplies help children in places where school supplies are scarce. Boxes with first aid supplies, soap, and toothbrushes help children learn health practices.

Boxes obtained through your local Red Cross chapter may be filled at any time during the school year, although the project is especially suited to holiday seasons, the beginnings of semesters, and when the need for helping disaster victims is high.

Program guidelines stress that each box should contain a variety of items. Among the educational materials recommended are pencils with erasers, box of crayons, small ruler, and a small pad of paper or notebook. A child size toothbrush, hand soap, small comb, or pocket size packet of tissues are preferred health items. Personal or recreational treats can include yo-yos, barrette or hair ribbon, harmonica, small puzzle, or marbles. Or students may want to make items like finger puppets and bookmarks. The addition of an attractive card, preferably handmade, expressing friendship is also encouraged. Filled boxes are delivered to a local Red Cross chapter for shipping.

The Red Cross sponsors a similar activity for high school students called the School Chest Program. A standard trunk or box can be used, or industrial arts students can make one as a classroom project. Each filled chest should contain basic health, school, and recreational supplies for a class of twenty-four students.

A third service activity sponsored by the Red Cross is the International Album Exchange Program, which provides school and youth groups an opportunity to communicate with young people in other countries served by the Red Cross. Through the program, young people can present life in their home, school, Red Cross group, community, and nation in a graphic manner. The sharing of ideas through artwork, photographs, stamps, crafts, tape recordings, written materials, and other album contents contributes both to greater friendship and better understanding among youth around the world. Likewise, albums prepared by young people from other Red Cross and Red Crescent groups in countries help students in the U.S. gain a better insight into their way of life.

You Can Do It

Complete guidelines, instructions, and shipping boxes for the Friendship Box program are available through your local Red Cross chapter. A package of twenty-five empty boxes costs $4.50. The Friendship Box Program is especially suited for elementary school students, but any young person, individually or as part of a group, can take part.

Request additional resource materials and program guidelines directly from your local Red Cross chapter.

SPONSOR A NEEDY CHILD

In January 1989, Robin Della, a fourth grader from Rushville, New York decided she wanted to help at least one hungry child eat better by becoming a sponsor through World Vision International.

"When I wake up in the morning I usually watch television," explains Robin. "And a commercial came on asking people to sponsor a needy child. My dad was in the other room and I went and asked him if I could sponsor a child and he said if I was really interested to go ahead and call the number.

"I said, 'Me?' and he said yes—so I called the number. They asked me my name, address, phone number and my dad's name. He got on the other phone. Then they told me I'd get some information in about two or three weeks."

Though Robin had seen ads before about sponsoring hungry children, she isn't sure what prompted her to take action that particular morning. Asking her dad about it was okay, but making the phone call made her nervous. She didn't even have any money of her own to use since the family has a policy not to give allowances until the children turn ten. "Before I went to ask my dad, I just said to myself, 'I've got to help.' It makes me sad to think people are dying because they don't have enough to eat."

Robin's mother, Sharrie, says that neither she nor her husband wanted to discourage Robin, who is the oldest of their three daughters. "We've always stressed to the girls not to waste. As an educator I witness a lot of waste, particularly food at school. I see kids throwing it away like there's no tomorrow. It just makes me sick." To help Robin out, they decided to make sponsoring a child as a family project.

Though Robin doesn't contribute money directly to the family's monthly pledge of twenty-five dollars, she has been the one to write to the child her family sponsors through the program. How does she feel now that she's gotten involved? "I feel good," Robin says.

You Can Do It

Organizations that operate programs to support needy children overseas often allow sponsors to choose between a boy or a girl from a variety of locations and countries. Monthly sponsorship fees vary but generally range from about twelve to twenty-five dollars a month per child.

As a precaution, before agreeing to sponsor a child, ask the organization to send you more information about their program by mail. Request a financial report so you can see how much of your sponsorship money will go directly towards helping a needy child and how much goes toward paying administration costs. You might also want to compare information from one organization with another, or speak to someone who is already participating in a particular program.

To contact World Vision International the toll-free number is (800) 423-4200 (U.S.) and (800) 268-3950 (Canada).

Two similar programs include: Save the Children, (800) 453-8100, and Children International, 2000 E. Red Bridge Road, Box 419055, Kansas City, MO 64141. Other programs are often advertised in magazines and by direct mail.

AMIGOS DE LAS AMERICAS

Ecuador   June 17, 1987

Dear Mom, Dad, Leslie, and Eric,

I am so excited! I just found out (five minutes ago) where I am going to be living for the next six weeks! It is a little town called Guambolicán.

We have the most rural town in Bolívar province. There is no electricity, no water, no school...

Love, Dianne

Dianne Johnson of Boulder, Colorado is just one of thousands of teens and young adults who have traveled to Latin America as part of the Amigos de las Americas program, which celebrated its twenty-fifth anniversary in 1989. The goals of this group are to develop youth leadership, provide public health services in Latin America, and improve cross cultural understanding. The volunteers have provided more than eleven million health services in such areas as rabies vaccination of dogs, human immunizations, vision screening and eyeglass distribution, oral hygiene counseling, home improvement, and community sanitation.

Though some Amigos are as young as fifteen when they begin their initial training, Dianne, a two year veteran, was eighteen the first year she traveled to Latin America. Her job in a remote village 8,000 feet high in the Andes of Bolivár, Ecuador was in "community sanitation" which, she explains, is just a more polite term for "latrine construction." Five other Amigos lived and worked in her village of about thirty families. They came from Oregon, Iowa, Minnesota, Washington, DC, and Colorado. With the addition of the Amigos, the population of Guanbolicán grew to 125 people that summer.

Elena Metcalf, seventeen, of Boulder, also spent her first year in Ecuador. She claims the easiest part about being an Amigo is signing up. The hard part is actually doing it. "Coming up with the strength inside me to actually follow through, that I wasn't so sure about. I was scared," she says, "especially right before leaving. Even after six months of training you never quite get the feeling you're really going. Then suddenly you're on the plane."

During their training, Amigos learn first aid, Latin American customs of food, manner, and behavior, intensive Spanish, and the skills involved to complete their assigned project. Some of the projects, like immunizations and vision screening, Amigos carry out while working alongside a nurse or doctor supplied by the host country's ministry of health.

"I think we figured that I personally gave 1,000 shots," says Elena of her second year spent in Paraguay. "I worked

Volunteers in Amigos de las Americas work hard at improving the living conditions of the countries they visit. (Used by permission of Amigos de las Americas.)

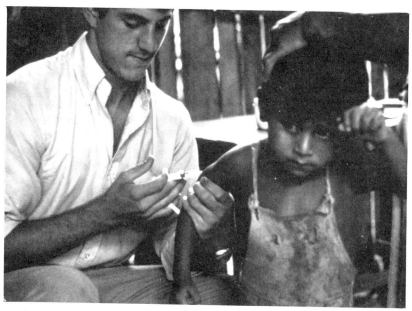

Amigos give children immunizations against disease. (Used by permission of Amigos de las Americas.)

with an Amigo partner and a nurse. We had two towns to cover, each with a number of rural communities around it. We went back for two doses. We had to arrange our own transportation. Sometimes we walked. Sometimes we talked villagers into giving us rides in whatever they were traveling on. It took us all of the summer." Their good Samaritan efforts weren't always appreciated, Elena admits. "Some parents didn't like the idea of us sticking needles into their kids."

For other projects, like latrine construction and home improvement, Amigos teach villagers the basic skills needed to complete the projects but will not do all of the work themselves. "It's important that they understand why sanitation is important and for them to be able to build new latrines as needed later," explains Elena.

Dianne adds, "Latrine construction is one of the most important programs, because it helps to break the disease cycle and save lives."

Amigos also spend a lot of time learning how to cope with the circumstances of the area in which they will live. The difference in food can cause intestinal upsets. The average diet of rice and beans, supplemented with native fruit and occasional meat, quickly grows almost unbearably boring for teens used to a steady dose of variety and junk food.

In many areas, water needs to be purified before drinking. Amigos carry iodine pills to purify the water then add citric acid or vitamin C to neutralize the bitter taste the iodine leaves.

Amigos are instructed on what clothing is acceptable, not just to endure the weather but also to avoid insulting or disturbing the local citizens. Faded or torn blue jeans and mini-skirts are out. Amigos are expected to present as professional an appearance as they can, given the circumstances. After all, they are representing the United States and are there to do an important job. Everyone is warned against wearing khaki colored clothing, especially camouflage, due to its association with military uniforms. Preparing for volunteer service in a program like the Amigos de las Americas takes more than just a sense of adventure and a willingness to reach out and share with the people of a foreign country. It takes commitment. You've got to do some deep soul searching. Not every Amigo makes it through the program.

"Some really can't handle a strange new culture and have to go home," says Sharon Metcalf, Elena's mother. The intense training helps weed out most of the teens for whom the experience would be just too much. Sharon estimates that only two or three Amigos out of 500 actually go home once they are in their host country. A few others may go home due to unexpected medical problems or the occasional accident.

Unfortunately, some potential Amigos never get a chance to even experience the training. Parents veto the project up front. "A lot of parents do have trouble letting their kids go halfway around the world," admits Elena, whose own path was cleared somewhat by her older brother Gabriel. He first found out about the program in his high school Spanish class and began as an Amigo a year before Elena.

Helen Johnson, Dianne's mother, says, "At first it was difficult to anticipate sending my daughter to a Latin American country to live in poverty! I was concerned about her safety, among other things."

Looking back, Mrs. Johnson still feels it was worth the risk despite her reservations. "Dianne is a very determined young lady. She was the kind of child that responded to a challenge. When I realized that she really wanted to do this we began to attend meetings where we talked to veteran Amigos and their parents. I learned that the Amigos organization is very concerned about safety. The decision on whether to have the program in a country is first based on safety of the volunteers, and there are well thought out plans to take care of emergencies.

"I also learned that Amigo volunteers gain a great deal from the experience. Dianne came home with much more confidence in herself. She has a whole new understanding of cultures other than our own. She learned so much about people and she gained many friends."

You Can Do It

Amigos de las Americas is a national organization that coordinates projects in several Latin American countries including Brazil, Mexico, Honduras, Costa Rica, and Paraguay. Volunteers, who include teens and young adults, are recruited and trained through area chapters which are usually sponsored by a local community service group. Since volunteers are responsible for their own costs, including airfare and personal supplies, volunteers participate in many fundraisers. Limited partial scholarships are also available.

For more information, contact the international office: Amigos de las Americas, 5618 Star Lane, Houston, TX 77057. Or call: (713) 782-5290, or (800) 231-7796. In Texas call: (800) 392-4580.

Many other organizations also sponsor international travel opportunities for young people. Minimum age restrictions vary, though there are some programs available for those as young as twelve or thirteen, especially through well established student exchange programs. Check with your minister or school counselor for help in locating exchange programs in your area.

Many young people participate in international programs by serving as hosts, instead of being exchange students themselves. Hosting an exchange student is also an excellent way for younger children to be involved in an international program.

NEW VIEWS

If you're interested in other countries, you may feel that you can't do much unless you can actually volunteer your time in a foreign country. If you want to fight world hunger, for instance, at this point in your life you probably won't be able to visit a developing country to teach new farming methods or to help distribute food.

But there are two important ways that you can help. One is to raise money for a group working on the problem that interests you. You'll find money raising ideas in Chapter 4.

The other very important way that you can help is to teach others about the problem. Here is just one example. In the late eighties, there was growing world concern over the slaughter of African elephants for their ivory. More and more people found out about the problem through newspaper and magazine articles, letters to the editor and even bumper stickers. Around the world, people put pressure on their governments to forbid traders from bringing ivory into their countries. Finally, in June 1989, all world trade ivory was banned. The elephants were given a second chance.

In a similar way, you can use your writing ability to make changes. A project called New Views, offered by Save the Children, can help. Each month New Views publishes *WorldWire*, a newsletter for teen journalists. It contains stories and story ideas, always with a local teen angle. Teens can then use these ideas as starting points to report on world issues in their school newspapers.

Janet McGinness, a high school senior from Independence, Missouri, is the editor of her high school newspaper. She has used *WorldWire* for ideas, even though many on the staff of her paper say that students are interested only in school events. Janet doesn't agree. "I think it's important for everyone to know what's going on in the world. I'd like to help world understanding." By taking part in a New Views workshop over the summer, Janet learned more about world issues and how to broaden the viewpoint of her news stories. She now works hard to show the effects a news event has on people's lives.

Janet learned that the best way to get student interest is to tie a world event to something familiar. A *WorldWire* story about child care in other countries led Janet to publish a similar story in her student paper. "Kids were interested because a lot of them are baby sitters."

Janet says, "Even if you think you can't make a difference, you still have to stick up for what you believe in. No matter what, I've got to make an effort to do what I think is right."

You Can Do It

WorldWire is published four times during the school year and is available from Save the Children, Public Affairs Department, 54 Wilton Road, Westport, CT 06880. Save the Children also offers other classroom programs as well as its well-known programs for sponsoring children around the world.

FOR MORE INFORMATION

American Institute for Foreign Study
102 Greenwich Avenue
Greenwich, CT 06830   (203) 869-9090

For junior high through college level students. Projects include homestays, cultural exchanges, and courses in continuing education.

American Red Cross — (see address page 76)

Amigos de Las Americas
5618 Star Lane   (713) 782-5290
Houston, TX 77057   (800) 231-7796
                          In Texas: (800) 392-4580.

Archaeological Excavations
Dept. of Antiquities & Museums
Museum of Education & Culture
P.O. Box 856
Jerusalem, 91004 Israel

Sometimes accepts volunteers as young as sixteen years old.

Civil Air Patrol
Maxwell Air Force Base
Alabama 36112   (205) 293-6019

Qualifying cadets can apply for the International Air Cadet Exchange, which sponsors projects in approximately twenty-one foreign countries each summer.

Write c/o Brig. Gen. Carl S. Miller USAF Ret., Administrator for more information. Cadet program itself is open to students in grade school through college and focuses on the social, cultural, economic, political, international, and vocational aspects of the aerospace field. Study courses are supplemented by practical experience in aviation, radio communication, weather observations, and by training in leadership skills, physical fitness, and character building.

Club De Vieux Manoir
10, Rudela Cossonnerie 75001
Paris, France

Open to those thirteen and over with three permanent sites in Guis, Argy, and Ponipoint. Costs involved. Write to the secretary's attention for application and brochure.

College Cevenol International
Work Camp Admissions Office
c/o Bill Brown
Box 68170
Brown University
Providence, RI 02912   (401) 272-5158 or (401) 751-2169

For ages seventeen to twenty-five. Service locations are in France. Applicants must have a least two years study of French.

Cooperative International
Pupil-to-Pupil Program
3229 Chestnut Street NE
Washington, DC 20018   (202) 529-2163

Arranges for students from ages six to eighteen to donate educational tools to their counterparts in Asia, Africa, and Latin America. Sends a composition book containing donor student's name, address, age, school, and a message of goodwill. Provides translation for letters received by U.S. students and helps to arrange embassy cooperation with participating.

Council on International Educational Exchange
205 E. 42nd Street
New York, NY 10017   (212) 661-1414
Co-sponsors educational exchange opportunities for high school students.

Earthwatch
680 Mount Auburn Street
Box 403 N
Watertown, MA 02272   (617) 926-8200
Must be sixteen or older; costs involved. Some scholarships available for students and teachers. Write for membership information. Projects are all environmentally oriented.

International Agricultural Exchange Association
58 Aboulevard
DK-2200 Copenhagen N
Denmark
Provides rural youth an opportunity to study agricultural practices in other countries through placement with host families on approved training farms. There are two types of exchange programs: (1) student spends six to eight months in one host country; (2) student spends six and a half months training in each of two host countries.

International Association of Volunteer Effort
10775 Wilkins Avenue #103
Los Angeles, CA 90024   (213) 470-1867
Members are interested in action through voluntary commitment to human service. Maintains an international bank of volunteer programs and an international network to encourage volunteer program development and to promote understanding through volunteer effort. Members include individuals from over forty nations.

Mobility International USA
P.O. Box 3551
Eugene, OR 97403   (503) 343-1284

Helps place people with disabilities in volunteer positions in both United States and abroad. Anyone over age fourteen may apply.

UNICEF
333 E. 38th Street
New York, NY 10016 (212) 686-5522

Encourages young people to take an active role in raising funds which are used to provide health care in developing countries. Projects include Trick or Treat for UNICEF and the Skip-a-Meal concept.

U.S. Student Travel Service
801 Second Avenue
New York, NY 10017 (212) 867-8770

Provides complete travel services for students, including summer jobs, homestays, language study, and special international tours and charter flights.

Youth for Christ/USA
Box 419
Wheaton, IL 60189 (312) 668-6600

Sponsors student exchange program.

Youth for Understanding
Student Exchange Program (800) 872-0200

Youth of All Nations
16 St. Luke's Place
New York, NY 10014 (212) 924-1358

Members, young people between ages fourteen to twenty-four, are put in touch with other "YOANers" and provided with a booklet of suggestions on how to begin and maintain correspondence for the purpose of developing world understanding and an appreciation for other nations and cultures. In the U.S., requests for information should include SASE. Has 11,000 members.

Additional Resources

International Directory of Youth Internships, by Cynthia R. Morehouse, available from Learning Resources in International Studies, Suite 9A, 777 United Nations Plaza, New York, NY 10017.

International Work Camps Directory, available from Volunteers for Peace, International Work Camps, Tiffany Road, Belmont, VT 05730.

Teenager's Guide to Study, Travel, & Adventure Abroad, available from Marjorie Adoff Cohen, CIEE, 809 United Nations Plaza, New York, NY 100017.

Volunteer Vacations and Volunteer Vacation Update, by Bill McMillan, 2120 Greenhill Road, Sebastopol, CA 95472.

12.

Extra Benefits of Volunteering

THE WARM FUZZIES

A friend of mine calls it "the warm fuzzies." It's that feeling you get when you know you've done a good deed without expecting anything in return. A tingly sensation spreads over your body and a blush rises to your cheeks and you suddenly find yourself grinning from ear to ear, especially when no one is looking.

Most of us feel comfortable admitting we enjoy a cozy dose of the warm fuzzies. But when it comes to admitting that our volunteer service might actually benefit us in other ways, then we start squirming in our seats and we become embarrassed just thinking about it, let alone talking about it out loud. It seems so uncharitable to think of ourselves. We feel selfish acknowledging that there might be any personal advantage to gain from volunteering.

OTHER BENEFITS

But most people, when they stop to think about it, will acknowledge that they have gotten some extra benefits from volunteering. Maybe they learned a new skill or discovered they had a knack for working with the elderly.

Still others, like Sue Lindsay, a member of the Law Enforcement Explorers, or Paul, a hospital youth aide, openly admit volunteering specifically to get some practical experience in the career they are thinking about pursuing. For them, the pleasure of participating in community service is an added benefit.

It's okay to acknowledge these extra benefits. By volunteering yourself to projects in which you can expect to develop your natural talents and interests, or in which there is an emotional or physical return, you'll be motivated to do and give your best. You'll care about more than getting the job done. And that's a major plus for both you and the people you serve.

Sometimes you know the extra benefits gained from lending a helping hand before you actually volunteer. Sometimes, except for warm fuzzies, you won't even be able to identify a benefit you gained until well after you're finished participating in a particular project. You may figure that out years later.

Thomas Garth, national director of the Boys Clubs of America, credits much of his success now as a business manager to what he learned as an active member of the St. Louis Boys Clubs, where he took a special interest in sports and community service projects as a youth. "Though I probably didn't realize it at the time, my Club experience provided me with a purpose and a direction."

Basically, there are five main areas in which you can benefit as a volunteer: financial, physical, spiritual, educational, and emotional. Frequently, a volunteer project will reward you in several of these ways. Let's take a look at them one at a time.

Financial Benefits

While volunteering usually won't pay you directly in funds you can put in the bank, volunteer work can often provide you with on the job training that you might otherwise not be able to afford. Later, you can use what you've learned to get a job or start your own sideline business. You might even advance to a paid job at the place you're volunteering.

For instance, if you do a lot of baby sitting, people might be willing to pay you more if they know you've completed a respected first aid course and spent two

This zoo volunteer is gaining self-confidence and knowledge through her presentations to zoo visitors. (Used by permission of the Audubon Zoological Garden.)

By planting tree seeds now, students are starting the forests of tomorrow. (Photo by Cathryn Berger Kaye. Used by permission of the Constitutional Rights Foundation.)

summers volunteering at a day care center. One teen advanced from volunteer work at her YMCA to a paid job there teaching music, tumbling, and reading.

If you have the time to volunteer but are short on money, you might be able to find a project that allows members money to help cover the costs of volunteer related expenses such as bus or subway fare and meals. You may also want to consider how a volunteer opportunity might save you money in the future. Suppose you're planning on a particular career. You may participate in the field as a volunteer and discover you don't really like working in the field at all. Money spent on learning that career would be a mistake. Sue Lindsay of the Sanilac County, Michigan, Law Enforcement program says that even though she still intends to pursue a career in some branch of law enforcement, her participation as an Explorer has made her realize how uncomfortable she feels in a potentially dangerous situation. "I know now I don't want to be a traditional cop."

Physical Benefits

If you enjoy playing a sport more than watching one, you might want to look into volunteer opportunities that require a lot of physical action. By reading the listings at the end of Chapter 9 you'll find out about all kinds of outdoor activities that need your help.

You can also look into possibilities to volunteer as an official, coach, or manager for a Little or Midget League sports team. You don't have to be a star player to be a coach or trainer. Mike Abdenour, head trainer for the Detroit Pistons Basketball Team, never super-athletic himself, was active on the sidelines throughout school by serving as a team manager or statistician. His early involvement helped him land the exciting job he has today.

And don't forget all the walk-a-thons, dance-a-thons, and other movements that are organized regularly to raise funds for such programs as the March of Dimes and muscular dystrophy. There are also walks to raise funds to feed the hungry and house the homeless. Check regularly in your local newspaper for a cause that is important to you.

By volunteering for projects that take some muscle and energy, you'll get healthy exercise at the same time that you're helping others.

Spiritual Benefits

Many religions encourage their members to participate in service to their religious and/or civic community. Service to others is an important part of many religions. You may want to find out about volunteer programs sponsored by your religious group. Many programs exist—Pirchei Agudath Israel and Bnos Agudath Israel for orthodox Jewish communities, the National Federation for Catholic Youth Ministry, the Royal Rangers Program of the Pentecostal Holiness Church, and many, many more.

Educational Benefits

Some volunteer agencies offer wonderful classes. They will make you a better volunteer and help you in the future, too. As Susan Walter of the American Red Cross points out, "If you take a course, you will be in an even better position to help out, especially in an emergency. Your Red Cross skills are also especially valuable if you plan on entering any of the medical-related fields when you graduate."

Since you are likely to learn new skills in any type of volunteer service you participate in, the real decision here depends on if you want to learn, or practice, a particular skill. Again, many of the health and public service related organizations offer a multitude of educational opportunities. If you feel bored or unchallenged, look for projects in areas you haven't tried before.

You may want to deliberately pursue volunteer activities that relate to future career plans. Or you may already possess skills in a field that you can share with others. Tutors are needed in many fields especially reading, writing, math, and science. You may want to volunteer through an organized program such as "Time to Read" or as a cadet teacher in your school. Or you may prefer just offering to study with a classmate or sibling who's having trouble keeping up. You may be surprised how teaching others helps you strengthen your own skills.

Emotional Benefits

At first glance, you may think the only benefit to weigh in this category is how many doses of warm fuzzies could you survive before overheating. But think again. Volunteering can offer great opportunities for emotional growth.

Many youth volunteers say that what they gained most from participating in community service projects was learning how to get along with others, as well as gaining a more realistic perspective about themselves and the people and world around them. Organizations stress that developing leadership skills is a prime benefit of volunteering.

Volunteering can also make you stronger emotionally. There are many areas of community service which can be gut wrenching experiences. Think of watching the homeless shuffle through a neighborhood soup kitchen day after day or helping children with leukemia. That's pretty strong stuff. You may not be ready for it quite yet.

On the other hand, you may handle things just fine, especially if you ease yourself into the situation slowly. Training programs will help you cope. They usually give you a chance to act out different difficult situations.

Your volunteer work may expose you to more suffering than you've seen before. But through it, you may gain compassion and the strength to work in difficult situations. Remember though, there is no shame in trying a program, then later deciding it's too much to handle.

Peer support groups can also offer emotional growth. You may be drawn to an emotional support or awareness group specifically because the topic in question has touched you personally. Sharing the anger, guilt, and loss of losing a loved one to a drunk driver isn't easy for members of Students Against Drunk Driving, but it does offer those who have experienced such situations a way to ease the pain and perhaps prevent it from happening to some one else. There are peer groups on nearly every subject imaginable, from living with cancer to struggling to stay in school until graduation. The reason is simple. No one can share insight into a problem better or offer more sincere support than a person who has been, or is going through it, personally.

MAKING THE DECISION TO UN-VOLUNTEER

Despite how it sounds, deciding to un-volunteer can be a positive rather than negative step in your development as a volunteer. If you've enjoyed your involvement thus far, bowing out, for whatever reasons, will be probably leave you feeling sad and even a bit lonely. You may suffer pangs of guilt. That's only natural and part of growing up.

The reasons for leaving are different for each volunteer, and only you can decide when it's the right time for you. You may be anxious to move on to new challenges. Or maybe you're just moving. Period. Sometimes, in reevaluating your participation you discover your priorities have changed. Robert N. Coons once said, "If the shoe fits, you're not allowing for growth."

When it's not change that makes you decide to leave, it's usually conflict. Maybe you couldn't be as active as you would have liked. Maybe you felt you just didn't fit in. Sometimes the personalities of various volunteers clash, and you decide it's not worth the trouble to resolve the personality differences. Not everyone can be friends.

Sometimes you can't understand why you feel the urge to leave. But if you are willing, occasionally, to let intuition alone guide you into a project, you must also be willing to let it guide you out.

However, don't go empty handed. Take what you've learned about giving and sharing with you. Remember the best times and the good things you helped accomplish. Then hold up your personal beacon and let it illuminate a new path for you to explore. There will be other volunteering possibilities around the bend.

A TRADITION OF GIVING

As a volunteer, you have become part of an American tradition of helping others, which was recognized over a century and a half ago by Alexis de Tocqueville. De Tocqueville was a Frenchman who came to America looking for the secret of our greatness. The secret, he decided, was in our people's enthusiasm for learning, sharing, volunteering, caring, and helping their neighbors.

Volunteerism and community service are not unique to America, but they do seem to flourish here in a way that the people of other countries have never quite been able to duplicate, or even understand. "You are always having dinners and parties to raise money for charity," a lady from the Russian diplomatic corps once said. "In the Soviet Union nobody does anything for strangers unless they get paid."

Modern American presidents, both Democrats like Jimmy Carter and Republicans like Ronald Reagan, continue to applaud American volunteers for their tireless efforts. When running for the Presidency, President Bush likened American volunteers to "A thousand points of light" and continues to call volunteerism "our greatest gift."

As a young volunteer, you are one of the many "thousand points of light" that George Bush was referring to. Your energy, your light, your help, does makes a difference. What would we do without you?

Index

3700

361.3
HEN
c 1

Henderson, Kathy.

What would we do
without you?

21095

$6.95

DATE			